MW00887987

Minecraft Stories Anthology

– Minecrafting Steve

Books 1-3

by

Funny Comics

Other Books In This Series

Special Bonus

Be sure to read to the back of the book for information on how to get FREE Kindle comics from Funny Comics!

Be sure to "LIKE" our Funny Comics Facebook Page by clicking below

https://www.facebook.com/FunnyComics3000

Subscribe to Funny Comic's YouTube channel here

Funny Comics YouTube Channel

https://www.youtube.com/channel/UC61rZRtwDl79i gc5ltb1Hcg/videos

Be sure to watch our epic Star Wars / Minecraft Mashup "Attack On The Death Square!"

Book 1 – Zombies Don't Eat Chicken

Day 1

Dear Journal,

It's me, Steve. I mean, who else would it be, right? Anyway. I finally arrived at my new home today—or at least the place that I hope I'll be able to call home. It's too soon to tell, since I just got here. Someone once told me that writing things down makes them easier to remember, and I don't want to forget any detail about my new adventure, so I've decided to keep you, journal. I'll try to write in you every day, though I can't promise anything.

I know, I know; it clearly says "Diary" on the front. But I think "journal" sounds more official, like I'm on an expedition or something. Which I am, kind of; I'm exploring a new part of the world, and while it's sort of scary, it's also exciting.

Anyway, like I said, I got here today. It took a long time to get here, and when I left, I wasn't sure where "here" would be. I just kind of wandered for a while. And then when I found "here," something about the place spoke to me. I mean, it didn't *actually* speak to me. I just felt like this is where I should be right now.

But here's the thing about "here": It's a little boring. Don't get me wrong, all the people here are *super* nice. It's just that... how do I describe it? Flat. Everything is flat. All the land is flat, as far as you can see. And even though there's a little village here, all the buildings are gray cubes. No kidding, every house and market and even the little motel they have (where I'm currently writing this) is just four gray walls and a flat gray roof. There are no signs anywhere, so I don't even know how the people here tell the buildings apart! If I wandered through the village, I probably wouldn't be able to find this building again. It looks like every other one.

So why would I, Steve, choose this place to call my new home? I'll tell you why, and it has to do with why I left that *other* place. I'm not going to go into details—I could fill a whole other journal with that story. Let's just say that I left because I wanted to be more creative.

See, more than anything else in the whole world, I want to be a builder. Not just any builder; I want to be a *great* builder. Where I come from, I was considered an okay builder, but I wasn't allowed to really be as creative as I wanted to be. So I left, and after wandering for a while, I got "here." And I hope that I can help turn this place into something awesome.

Sure, I could have chosen to start fresh with an empty field or something. But I like being around people, and I could probably use some help. I'm thinking of this little village like a blank slate, or an empty canvas, and when I'm done, it'll be a real work of art!

…Or at least I hope so.

Anyway, that's about it for now, journal. I'm going to get some sleep, because tomorrow is going to be the start of this new adventure!

Day 2

Dear Journal,

Okay, I'm starting to think that "dear journal" doesn't sound quite as good as "dear diary." Even though I like "journal" better, "dear diary" just has a certain ring to it.

Anyway.

Today was a big day, and I have a lot to tell you! Some pretty amazing stuff happened. I started my morning by telling the people of the village that I wanted to stay. They were very welcoming, and even the mayor of the town, a very nice man with a funny little beard, came out to greet me. Everyone calls him Mr. Mayor, though I doubt

that's his real name. Mr. Mayor offered me one of their

little gray cube houses to live in, but I said, "No thanks.

I'm going to build my house."

Of course, when I said that, all the people in town started whispering to each other, like they'd never heard of anyone doing such a thing. They must have a builder somewhere among them, or maybe someone came along and built all these little gray cube houses for them and then left. I don't know. Either way, they were very curious.

I wanted to make sure I had a lot of space to build, so I went outside the town limits and picked a big open area in the field. And I started building.

I began with a layer of cobblestone as a foundation, and then built up the walls with wood planks. I put glass panes in for windows, and a red front door (for a little bit of color). As I was building, some of the people from the town started to gather around to watch.

Now, I have to admit, the type of house that I was building was pretty basic. I just wanted a little cabin that I could call home while I worked on my *real* project (which

I'll tell you about a little later). But all these people from the town thought my cabin was the greatest thing they ever saw!

And when I started building the stairs to the second floor, they gasped.

One man came forward. I think he was the owner of the pizzeria (though I couldn't really tell you which building the pizzeria was, since they all look the same), and he said, "What are *those* for?"

I just kind of stared at him for a while. I mean, how do you explain stairs to somebody? Then I realized that all of their little gray cubes were one-story buildings. There wasn't a stair in the whole village.

I almost laughed, but I didn't want anyone to feel bad, so I calmly told them, "These are stairs. They're used to get to the second floor."

The crowd gasped again. "*Second* floor?" they said. "You can put another floor on top of the first one?"

Okay, I have to admit, this time I did laugh a little. "Of course you can! Where I come from, there are buildings that are thirty or forty floors tall!"

People began talking excitedly, and one woman actually fainted. Can you believe that?

So I kept building, and these people kept watching. It was like they forgot all about their lives and jobs and whatever else they had to do, they were so fascinated by my little cabin.

And I thought to myself, *If you think this is cool, just wait and see!*

As the sun went down, I decided to pause work on my cabin, at least for now. I still have to finish the second floor, and there's no roof, but it's a nice night and I can see all the stars, so that's okay with me.

And wouldn't you know it? Right after I went through my new red front door and settled in for bed, Mr. Mayor came and knocked. He had a few other people from the village, and when they saw the inside, they looked around for a while, not saying anything.

Then Mr. Mayor told me, "Steve, you're obviously a very talented builder. This is the best house we've ever seen! And... well... we would really love it if you built some other things for us, too."

Jackpot! At least that's what I wanted to say. But instead I smiled and calmly said, "Mr. Mayor, that would be great."

So tomorrow I'm going to finish my cabin, and then I start my new job, as the village builder!

Day 5

Dear ~~Journal~~ Diary,

Okay, I give up. "Dear diary" does sound much better. And dear diary, I am *exhausted*. I know, I skipped a couple of days of writing, but I've been so busy that I couldn't even hold a pen. Let me explain:

I finished my cabin, and then I went to see Mr. Mayor about fixing up some other stuff. I asked him what he wanted me to do.

He just kind of looked at me funny for a long moment, and then he said, "Well... what do you think we should do?"

See, he had no idea what he wanted me to do! Don't get me wrong, these people are all very nice, but they were looking to me for answers. They were telling me I could do whatever I wanted.

On the one hand, I was really excited. This was exactly what I had hoped it would be: the chance to do something really creative and fun and big. Rebuild a whole village, that's big, right? On the other hand, though, I was a little nervous. Okay, I was a *lot* nervous, because I had never really been a decision-maker before. No one had ever asked me, "What do you think we should do?"

Even though I was really nervous, I couldn't show it. These people were looking to me for answers, so I would give them answers, even if that meant hiding my nervousness and pretending I had a plan.

"Well, Mr. Mayor," I said, "I think we should start at the center and work our way to the outskirts. We'll rebuild each building as we come to it." I thought that was a pretty good idea, and as the words came out of my mouth, more ideas came into my mind. "And we'll build cobblestone streets. And small sloping hills, so that everything's not flat. And we'll put all the shops and markets downtown, and all the houses uptown. And..."

And the ideas just kept coming. When I was finally done, Mr. Mayor laughed. At first I thought he was laughing at me, but then he hugged me—no kidding, he actually hugged me—and said, "All of your ideas are fantastic! Yes, yes, and yes! Let's start right away!"

What I *didn't* know was that when Mr. Mayor said "Let's get started," what he really meant was that *I* should get started, because no one else in the whole village knew how to build.

So I got started.

I knew I should have had a plan, like blueprints or a drawing or something, but I decided to just go for it and see what happened. The village people were impressed by my cabin, so I was sure that whatever I thought up would be pretty amazing to them.

I thought that the center of the town should have something big and interesting, so that travelers would have something to see that would catch their eye. After thinking about it for a short while, I decided on a clock tower. It would have to be tall enough to see from afar, so I settled on four stories.

And I started building.

I made it with white walls and a red roof and a big clock face in the front so that everyone would always know what time it was just by looking up. I put winding stairs inside so that anyone could walk up and look out over the town. The problem was, the clock face was bigger than me, and I needed some help to get it up there.

Then something weird happened.

I asked, but no one would help me. It turns out that *everyone* in this whole town is afraid of heights! At first I thought that was kind of weird, but then I remembered that fear of heights is one of the most common fears there is. And these people were used to living in little one-story buildings. It made sense.

I've never been afraid of heights. In fact, I love looking down from something high, like a tree or a rooftop. But lots of people are afraid of tall places. That's called taking something for granted, when you believe that other people look at something the same way you do. I was taking it for granted that these people would think like me and enjoy the height of the tower. It's not usually good to take things for granted. For example, the people in the village took it for granted that I was a great builder and wasn't at all nervous, when really I was. There are things that I'm afraid of that other people might not be. I won't go into them here, because I'll just creep myself out if I talk about them, but trust me, there are plenty of things I'm scared of!

Well, I struggled with the clock face for a long time, but I managed to get it up there. And when I came back down, the entire village had gathered around the base of the clock tower. Maybe they didn't want to be up at the top looking down, but they really liked being at the bottom looking up! They congratulated me and smiled and laughed. It was the best thing they'd ever seen.

I even got a free pizza out of it, which is my favorite food ever (right next to hot dogs)!

Mr. Mayor patted me on the back and said, "Nice job, Minecraft Steve." That's what he called me: Minecraft Steve.

Since then, other people in the village have been calling me that too. I've always just been "Steve," but hey, I don't mind the new name at all. In fact, I think it's pretty great.

Now excuse me, diary, I've got to get some sleep.

There's another big day ahead tomorrow!

Day 10

Dear Diary,

I met a chicken today. I know that sounds weird, but he's actually a really nice guy… or, chicken.

Sorry I skipped a few days again. I've just been so busy! After building the clock tower, I laid a cobblestone courtyard around it, and then started working on the streets and some of the surrounding buildings. The one thing that the villagers can help me with is taking apart the old gray cube buildings, so that made a little less work for me, but rebuilding them all from scratch was more than I bargained for!

After the third or fourth building, I started running out of new ideas. I wanted each building to be a little different from the others, but I was having some trouble being original with every new design. I knew what I really needed to do.

See, where I came from, one of the best things to do when you needed to do some thinking was to take a walk and be alone for a little while. Ever since I started building here, all the villagers would come by at all hours of the day to see my progress and to "ooh" and "ah" over my new creations. I really needed some Minecraft Steve thinkin' time, so I took a break from building and walked.

Like I mentioned before, the whole village is totally flat, and the land around the village is flat, like a big field in all directions (which I hoped to change soon). But beyond that, to the north, there was a forest, so I decided to walk there. There's something pleasant about trees, the way they look and smell, that always makes me feel better.

So I walked to the edge of the forest, and just as I was about to go in, a voice said, "You don't want to go in there!"

I stopped and looked around. Nearby, where the field met the trees, was a white chicken a little taller than my knee. "What did you say?" I asked him.

He pecked the ground twice and then said, "You don't want to go in there! There are wolves in those woods."

"Cool," I said, and I started to walk into the woods.

"Hey!" cried the chicken. "Aren't you scared?"

"Nah," I said. "I've met wolves before. They're pretty nice, when you get to know them. Hey, I might even have a bone with me somewhere." I checked my pockets as the chicken moved closer to me. He was looking at me funny, with his head tilted to one side.

"What?" I asked him.

"You're that new builder. The one that's not afraid of heights."

"Yeah, so?" I asked him.

"And you're not afraid of wolves either?" the chicken said.

"Wolves only attack if you attack them first," I explained.

The chicken looked at me for a long time, and then he finally said, "I'm Charlie. Can I walk with you?"

See, diary, where I come from, "chicken" means two things. It can mean "a flightless domestic bird," which Charlie was. Or it could also mean "someone who is cowardly or timid," which Charlie also was. Charlie was a chicken in both senses of the word.

I'm not being mean to Charlie; I'm just telling it like it is. He walked with me in the woods, telling me a little about himself, but every time a bird chirped or something rustled in the leaves, Charlie jumped in fright, flapping his wings a couple of times and shedding feathers.

Just like the people in the village, Charlie is afraid of heights (which I thought was weird for a bird, but then again, chickens don't fly). Charlie is also afraid of the woods, because of the wolves. But that's not all. Charlie is afraid of water, because he can't swim. Charlie is afraid of balloons, because they might pop at any second. Charlie is afraid of new people, because they might try to eat him. Charlie is afraid of...

Well, you get the idea. Charlie's afraid of a lot of things. And hearing about all of Charlie's fears made me realize something. I'm not proud of it, but at first I wanted to laugh at Charlie for being afraid of so many ridiculous things. But then I realized that I was taking it for granted that other people (or chickens) shouldn't be afraid of something just because I wasn't afraid of that thing. Who knows? Maybe the things that I find scary wouldn't frighten Charlie at all.

Learning about Charlie's fears did turn out to be a good thing, though, because it made me feel more confident, and I was ready to go back to building. I also had another idea.

"I like you, Charlie," I said to the chicken as we left the woods. "How about this: why don't you come help me build, and when we need a break, we'll work on some of your fears? Maybe I could teach you how to swim, or how to tame a wolf."

Charlie had to think about it for a little while, but eventually he agreed. "Okay, Steve. That sounds good to me."

And just like that, I made my first real friend.

Day 14

Dear Diary,

Today was terrifying. I'm not even sure I can write about why. That's how scary it was. So instead, I'll write some other stuff that's been happening in the last few days, to try to take my mind off of how completely frightened I am.

Charlie is a great assistant. I mean, he can't really help me build, because he has wings instead of arms and feathers instead of fingers, but he's great at conversation, so he keeps me company. He also has some really good ideas, and he helps me stay original (except the idea to put a statue of a chicken in the clock tower courtyard. I don't think that one's going to fly. No pun intended!).

Every day, we take a break and we walk into the woods to help Charlie get over his fear of the wolves. We've seen them twice now, and just like I promised, the wolves keep their distance and ignore us—if we don't mess with them, they don't mess with us.

I dug a small pit just outside of town and filled it with water for Charlie to learn how to swim. So far he can only doggie-paddle (or chicken-paddle?) but he's getting there. With each new lesson, I dig the pit a little bit deeper, and now Charlie's feet can't even touch the bottom, and he still manages to stay afloat! I think it won't be long until he's swimming like a pro.

And that's the second reason that Charlie is such a great assistant—and friend. See, diary, since Charlie has all these fears that I take for granted, it makes me feel braver and more confident. And because I'm helping Charlie get over his fears (or at least some of them), he's feeling braver and more confident every day too. It's been really great.

…Until today, anyway. But I still don't think I can talk about that yet.

The people in the town continue to be really grateful for all the work that me and Charlie are doing, and as a reward, they make sure that we always have bacon pizza whenever we want it. (See, Charlie's favorite food is bacon, and mine is pizza, so pizza with bacon on it was a good compromise.)

The town is really starting to shape up nicely. Almost half of it is rebuilt now, and we've made enough progress that I've started to think about what else I want to build when the town is finished.

Remember earlier, when I mentioned my *real* project? The cabin was just a warm-up. The town is getting better all the time. But what I really want to build is a castle of my very own. That's right, diary, you heard me: a castle! With a moat and a drawbridge and a courtyard and towers… just like the ones in medieval times. That's my ultimate goal. And after that, who knows?

For now, I've got my little cabin, and I even built a small addition on the side of it for Charlie. (I called it a "chicken coop," but Charlie insists on calling it "the guest house," even though it's too small for anything bigger than a chicken to actually fit inside.)

Okay, diary, I think that's enough writing for today. I'm going to get some sleep… if I can.

Day 14 (part 2)

Dear Diary,

I can't sleep.

I tried, but I'm still too freaked out to sleep. It's well past midnight now, and the later it gets, the more I think about it. Maybe writing it down will help. Here goes:

Earlier today, a Creeper wandered into the village.

Now, I just want to point out that I'm not scared of Creepers. There are all sorts of creatures in Minecraft, and most of them aren't scary, just like I don't think the wolves are scary. Most people find Creepers creepy, but I just think they're annoying. The way I see it, as long as they're not blowing up anything I've built, I don't really mind them.

But everyone else in the village lost their minds!

Just the sight of this Creeper had people scurrying all over the place, running this way and that, shouting, "Creeper! Run for your lives, it's a Creeper!" I tried to shout back at them to tell them that as long as no one gets near it, it'll be okay, but they were too busy being scared out of their wits to listen.

Well, I had planned ahead for something like this. On my second day of building, I had asked Mr. Mayor to get an ocelot. He didn't even ask me why; he just made sure to get one. We kept it in a big pen behind the courtyard to the clock tower, and when this Creeper wandered into town and everyone else was busy losing their heads, I calmly went over and let the ocelot out of its pen.

It chased the Creeper right out of town! No one was harmed, and nothing was blown up. Once everyone calmed down, I explained that Creepers flee from ocelots, and as long as we kept at least one, we had nothing to worry about.

Well, diary, you would have thought I saved the world! The villagers cheered for me and chanted my name, "Minecraft Steve! Minecraft Steve!" It was about the best thing that ever happened to me—and I didn't really do anything. The ocelot did all the work.

But that wasn't the scary part.

See, after we were done celebrating, Charlie and I decided to take the rest of the day off and enjoy a bacon pizza. As we were eating, Charlie casually said, "At least it wasn't a zombie."

And I stopped chewing. My slice of pizza fell out of my hand. I must have been staring at him, because he said, "What's up, Steve?"

And I muttered, "Did you say... zombie?"

"Yup," Charlie said. "There's a cave in the woods that's infested with them. They don't normally mess with us, but every once in a while a few of them will wander into the village."

Zombies. Real zombies live in a cave near the village that I now call home.

You see, diary, where I come from, there were no zombies—at least not that I ever saw. I didn't even think they were real. I thought they were just made-up stories to scare kids. But even the *stories* about them were terrifying.

A wolf might bite you. A Creeper might blow up. But a zombie is the worst of them all, because a zombie will turn you into another zombie, and then you'll be nothing more than a gross greenish thing, shambling around and moaning "oooohhhh, uuuuhhhh" as you search for other people to turn into zombies.

As a kid, I thought that was the scariest thing I'd ever heard.

Until today, of course, when I learned that zombies are very real, live close to me, and sometimes wander into the village. Now *that's* the scariest thing I've ever heard, and I can't sleep, because I keep thinking that a zombie is going to come banging on my door, or come crashing through my window, or I'll wake up and there will be one in my bedroom and it'll be breathing on me and moaning, "uuuuuhhhh…"

Okay, diary, I need to calm down. I'm just creeping myself out even more. Tomorrow, I'll talk to Charlie and try to find out some more information about these zombies.

Tonight, I'll try to get at least a little sleep. With the lights on.

Day 15

Dear Diary,

I had a plan for today. My plan was that while I was building, I would casually ask Charlie about the zombies. I'd ask him what they looked like, and if they really smelled as bad as the stories said they did. I would ask him how often they came into the village, and most importantly, I would ask him if they really did turn people into fellow zombies.

That was my plan, anyway. But I couldn't do that, because Charlie wasn't around.

I have no idea where he is. I mean, he doesn't *have* to always help me build. We don't pay him in anything but bacon pizza, so if he wanted to do something else, he's allowed to. I just wish he would have told me he wasn't going to be here, because I really wanted to get more information on the zombies.

My skin is crawling just thinking about them.

I didn't get much building done today without Charlie around. I also kept looking over my shoulder, thinking I was going to see a horde of zombies come shambling up the street. Twice a villager came to talk to me and I jumped in fright.

I really need to get it together, diary. The people here look up to me. They think I'm the bravest person they've ever met. I'm supposed to be a hero to them. I can't let them know that I'm afraid of anything.

That's all for today, diary. I'm sure Charlie will be back tomorrow.

Day 16

Dear Diary,

Okay, now I'm getting worried. Not only did Charlie not show up again today, but he wasn't in the chicken coop—sorry, the "guest house"—last night either. Where could he be?

I'm way too distracted to build. Something bad could have happened to Charlie, and as his friend, it's up to me to find out.

Day 17

Dear Diary,

Well, it's official. I am a coward. I'm a big ol' chicken. From now on, they can call me Chicken Steve, instead of Minecraft Steve.

I took the day off from building, which Mr. Mayor wasn't too happy about, since I'm only halfway done with his office, but I really need to find Charlie. He still hasn't shown up.

I spent all afternoon going from door to door and asking every villager if they've seen him. No one had. Finally, I asked the butcher, and he said, "No, I haven't seen him lately, but two days ago he came and asked me for a bone. I don't know why."

Now that was weird. What would Charlie want with a bone? He's a chicken. He doesn't like bones. I thought and thought, and then I realized what must have happened. When me and Charlie first met, I told him that a wolf could be tamed with a bone. Charlie must have been decided that the best way to get over his fear of the wolves was to try to tame one.

Normally, I would think that was a very good idea, and a great way for Charlie to get over his fear… except that to tame a wolf, he'd have to go into the woods. The woods that had a cave in them. A cave that had zombies in it.

I ran out of the town and through the field and came to the edge of the forest. Sure enough, I found a single white feather stuck to a tree. Charlie was here. I called out for him several times, but there was no answer.

Charlie must have gone into the woods, and something terrible could be happening to him right now!

But like I said before, I'm just as much of a chicken as Charlie, because I couldn't go into those woods. The sun was getting low, and it would have been dark soon. I'm not scared of the dark, but there was no way I'm going into those zombie-filled woods at night.

Poor Charlie. He thought he had a brave friend, and that made him feel brave. But he doesn't have a brave friend. He just has a friend that pretends to be brave.

Day 18

Dear Diary,

I didn't leave the house today. If someone hadn't knocked at the door, I probably would not have even left my bed today.

I felt like a fraud, a big phony. All of these people here looked at me like I was fearless, and here I was hiding in my cabin when my friend needed my help. By this point, I was sure that Charlie was beyond saving. It had been three days since he disappeared. So instead of being brave and going out there and finding my friend, I laid in bed and felt sorry for myself.

Until, like I said, someone knocked on my door.

It was Mr. Mayor. I thought he would be angry at me because I had still left his office half-finished, but instead he looked worried. I invited him in and he sat down in a chair and stared at me.

"What's wrong, Steve?" he asked me.

At first I didn't want to tell him, but it felt good to talk to someone, so I told him the whole story. Well, most of it. I told him about Charlie disappearing, and how he took a bone from the butcher and went into the woods to tame a wolf, and how he hadn't come back, and that I assumed that the zombies had gotten him.

I left out the part that I was terribly, horribly, teeth-chatteringly afraid of the zombies.

"I see," Mr. Mayor said. He stroked his pointy beard and said, "That *is* bad news. But maybe not all bad."

"What do you mean?" I asked.

"Well, if the zombies got him, then I'm sure by now he is a zombie too," Mr. Mayor said. My heart sank at the thought of a zombie Charlie. And then a chill went down my spine as I realized that Charlie the Zombie Chicken might come and try to turn me into a zombie! Now *that* was a scary thought.

"However," Mr. Mayor went on, "it's not *all* bad news. There is, perhaps, one thing that could be done."

"What?" I asked eagerly.

"There is an item that can cure zombification, a golden apple. If someone had the golden apple and fed it to a zombie, they would become a regular person again—or in this case, a regular chicken."

"A golden apple!" I jumped to my feet, suddenly filled with hope. "Well, where are they? Where can I find one?"

"Unfortunately, there's more bad news," said the mayor. "There is only one that I know of around here, and… well… the zombies have it. They have hidden it in their cave so that we cannot turn any zombies back into villagers."

"Oh," I said, and my heart sank again. The hope was gone again.

"But!" said Mr. Mayor suddenly, "I imagine that someone who is brave, and a true friend, and is very creative, could retrieve the golden apple, and their zombie friend, and turn him back into a regular person again." Mr. Mayor cleared his throat. "Sorry, a regular chicken."

"But I…" I started to say. I didn't want to admit that I wasn't as brave as everyone thought I was.

Mr. Mayor stared at me for a long while. I stared out the window, hoping that I didn't look scared.

"You know," he said, "as the mayor, my job is to lead this village, and I've been mayor for a long time. I call every villager my friend. Sometimes my friends need my help. And sometimes the thing that must be done is scary, even to me. It's perfectly natural to feel fear. It can't be helped. But overcoming those fears, especially to help someone in need, is what really makes someone a hero." Mr. Mayor stood up. "And sometimes the things we're afraid of aren't quite as scary as they seem." He smiled at me, and then he left.

I couldn't believe it. Mr. Mayor could tell that I was afraid, even though I didn't say it. And it didn't seem like he thought any less of me. He didn't try to make me feel bad. He was right; Charlie needed my help, and afraid or not, I was going to help him.

I grabbed a bag and starting packing some things that I would need. Tomorrow, diary, I'm going to get my friend back!

Day 19

Dear Diary,

I'm writing this entry from the top of a tree. Why am I in a tree? Why did I bring my diary? Well, I'll tell you. But first let me go back to this morning.

I woke up early, grabbed my bag, and headed toward the woods. I wanted to get there while it was still daylight. I packed some apples (in case I needed a snack), a blanket (in case I had to spend the night in the woods), a bone (in case I had to distract any wolves), a couple of firecrackers (in case I needed a distraction), a pickax (in case I had to fight off any zombies, even though the idea of having to use it was very scary), and you, diary.

I thought I was well prepared, but the one thing that I didn't think of was that I had no idea where the zombie cave was. I was already deep into the woods before I realized that I probably could have asked Mr. Mayor how to get there, if he even knew. But it was too late for that; I had already come too far.

It took me a *long* time to find the cave. In fact, I found two other caves first. The first one was a den of wolves. They weren't terribly interested in me, but they were a little unhappy that I had barged into their cave, so I tossed them the bone and went on my way.

The second cave was empty... or so I thought at first. After wandering around in the darkness for a while, I heard a hissing sound and I knew right away that I had stumbled into a Creeper cave, so I ran out of there as fast as

I could. The Creepers chased me, so I tossed my firecrackers over my shoulder and they went off with a loud *BANG!* The Creepers thought that other Creepers were exploding, so the ones that were chasing me blew up too. Luckily I managed to get away in time.

It was nearly night time before I found the zombies' cave. I knew it was the right cave because of the smell. Boy, did they smell bad! I guess the stories were right about that.

And then I saw one.

It looked like a person, except that its skin was green and its eyes were black. It didn't really shamble— you know, that slow, shuffling walk that you always hear about zombies. No, this one just kind of... walked around, but with its arms out in front of it.

That's about all I noticed about it before I hid. Just seeing that thing was so frightening that my legs temporarily stopped working. They felt like jelly, but after a few moments, I managed to get them working again. I made sure that the zombie didn't see me, and then I scrambled up into the nearest tree as fast as I could.

I climbed up high enough that I was sure the zombies couldn't see me. (And even if they could, I had no idea if zombies could climb trees or not.) And I watched. And what I saw amazed me.

The first zombie was walking around the front of the cave when a second zombie came out. He looked at the first zombie and said, "See anything, Bob?"

No kidding. The zombie *talked*.

And the first zombie—apparently named Bob—talked back. "Nope. Nothing out here."

"Good," said the second zombie. "Last time those wolves came around, one of them ran off with Joe's arm."

The second zombie went back into the cave, leaving Zombie Bob to continue his patrol.

I couldn't believe what I was hearing. The zombies could speak. They had names, maybe even the same names they had when they were people.

And most importantly, they seemed to be afraid of the wolves!

It makes sense, right, diary? Everyone is afraid of something. I'm afraid of the zombies, but not of the wolves. The zombies are afraid of the wolves, but not of me. And the wolves are afraid of me, but not of the zombies.

Knowing this made the zombies a little less scary. But just a little. I still had no doubt that they would turn me into a zombie if they caught me, and I didn't want any wolves to run off with my arms. So I waited, and I watched Zombie Bob pace outside the cave.

I've been up in this tree for about two hours now, watching the entrance to the cave. I munched on a couple of apples and wrapped my blanket around me, because it's getting kind of cold.

So let's go back to the beginning of this entry: why did I bring you along, diary? Well, because as soon as Zombie Bob goes away, I'm going into that cave. I'm going to get that golden apple, and I'm going to find Charlie the Zombie Chicken, and I'm going to un-zombify him.

Well, I'm going to try, anyway. If I succeed, I'll write all about my adventure tomorrow.

If I fail, this will be my last diary entry, and hopefully someone else will find this diary and know what happened to me and Charlie!

Day 20

Dear Diary,

Uuuuhhhhh…. Ooooohhhhh… Brrraaaaiiiinnns…

Ha, just kidding, diary. That's what I would have written if I was Zombie Steve now instead of Minecraft Steve. But I'm still me, which means that I did *not* get turned into a zombie. In fact, I'm writing this from the comfort of my cabin, safe and warm indoors.

However, I did not steal the golden apple *or* find Zombie Charlie. But I also sort of did.

Let me explain:

After a while, Zombie Bob left his guard post and went back into the cave. I climbed down from the tree. I *really* didn't want to go inside the zombies' cave at night, but I didn't see any other choice. It was a dark cave. It wouldn't matter if I went in the daytime or at night, right?

So in I went.

The cave was wide enough for a few people to walk side-by-side, and every now and then there were big stalagmites, which are rock formations that rise up from the floor, so I had something to hide behind. I hid behind a stalagmite, and then I checked to see if the coast was clear. Then I ran to the next stalagmite, and checked again. And then I ran again.

This continued for a while, deep into the cave. As I ran, I did encounter a couple of zombies here and there, but not many, and none of them saw me.

That didn't make it any less scary, though. I knew that all it would take was one single zombie to notice me, and that would be the end! Somehow my legs kept working, even though my heart was pounding a mile a minute and I was shaking from head to toe.

The cave eventually widened, and I found myself in a huge room, even bigger than the castle I was planning to build. And there were zombies *everywhere*. Loads and loads of zombies in every corner of the room. There must have been a hundred zombies there!

And they were all talking to each other. Dozens of conversations were going on at once. It was really weird, considering how scary I thought the zombies were, to hear them just chatting with each other. Still, I really didn't want to get caught. I hid behind a stalagmite for a while, and after several minutes, I dared myself to peek out.

There it was. On the far side of the huge chamber, sitting on a pedestal made of rock, was the golden apple, shiny and bright. All I had to do was make it across the huge room filled with zombies.

Easy, right?

Like a ninja, I went from stalagmite to stalagmite, hiding for a few minutes at a time to catch my breath before I ran to the next one. The zombies were too busy chatting with each other to notice me. I guess they assumed that no one would be brave enough to just walk right into their cave.

I was there. I was hiding behind the pedestal. All I had to do was reach up and grab the golden apple. And I did… or at least I tried to. As I was reaching for it, a loud voice said, "Hey, who's that guy?"

And suddenly a hundred pairs of black eyes were on me.

Every voice in the chamber was suddenly quiet, and every zombie was staring at me. One zombie stepped forward (I think it might have been Zombie Bob, but I can't be sure; they sort of all look alike).

"Hey," said the zombie. "What do you think you're doing?"

I was caught. I swear I thought my heart stopped. But I had faced my fears up to that point, right? I tried not to let my voice sound shaky as I said, "I need this golden apple. And I need my friend back so that I can turn him back into a regular chicken."

"Chicken?" said the zombies. They looked at each other, confused. (At least I think they were confused. Zombies don't show a lot of expression.)

"We don't turn chickens into zombies," said another zombie.

"But... my friend Charlie..." I stammered. "He was lost in the woods... you didn't take him?"

"Charlie? Yeah, we have Charlie. But he's not a zombie," said the closest zombie.

"Huh?" was all I could say.

Several zombies stepped aside to show me that in one corner of the big room was a small group of baby zombies. And they were riding a chicken as if he was a horse.

Charlie! (See, I told you I didn't find Zombie Charlie. He wasn't a zombie after all!)

"Hey, Steve," Charlie said. "What are you doing here?"

"I came to rescue you!"

"Oh." Charlie smiled. "I don't need rescuing, though. These baby zombies just wanted to ride a chicken."

"See?" said Zombie Bob. "We don't turn chickens into zombies. We turn *people* into zombies!" And he took a big step forward with his arms out.

"Wait!" I cried. My mind raced. What could I say to a bunch of zombies to keep them from turning me into one?

"You'll like being a zombie," said Zombie Bob as he came even closer. Other zombies began to crowd around him, coming toward me in a mob.

"Um… uh…" *Think, Steve, think!* I said to myself desperately. Then it came to me. "The wolves!" I shouted.

Zombie Bob paused for a moment. "What about the wolves?"

"You're afraid of the wolves. But I know how to tame them! And I can teach you!"

Zombie Bob looked at the other zombies, and then back at me. "You can tame the wolves?"

"Yes, and I'll show you how! But you have to let me and Charlie go." Then I added, "And I want the golden apple."

The zombies thought about this for a moment, and then they huddled together and whispered for a while. Then Zombie Bob said to me, "Alright. If you can teach us how to tame the wolves, we'll let you and your friend go."

"Great!" I said. "I'll need a bone…"

So I did. I taught the zombies how to tame the wolves so that they weren't afraid anymore. And the zombies, true to their word, they let me and Charlie leave the cave. After all, the baby zombies didn't need to ride a chicken anymore; they had pet wolves. They even let us take the golden apple with us.

As we left, Zombie Bob waved goodbye and said, "We'll be seeing you again… *real* soon!"

That creeped me out, of course.

By morning, Charlie and I were back in the village. The people congratulated us on retrieving the golden apple, and we were hailed as heroes.

But really, we were exhausted, so we went back to the cabin.

"Thanks for saving me," Charlie said. "You're a true friend."

"My pleasure, pal," I said. "To be honest, I was a little freaked out by the zombies."

"Oh yeah?" Charlie said with a smile. "Are you saying that Minecraft Steve is afraid of something that Charlie the Chicken isn't?"

"Why would you be? They don't turn chickens into zombies."

Charlie stretched his wings and said, "No, but those baby zombies really gave me a backache. I'm beat."

"Me too."

Now if you'll excuse me, diary, I really need to get some sleep.

Day 22

Dear Diary,

Now that I'm well rested, it's back to business as usual. Mostly.

I finished building Mr. Mayor's office, which made him very pleased. We took some seeds from the golden apple and we planted a golden apple tree in the courtyard of the clock tower, right in the center of town, just in case the zombies come back. (I *really* didn't like how Bob said he'd see me again "real soon.")

I came here looking for an adventure, and I definitely found one. And I learned a thing or two. I learned that being afraid doesn't make me a chicken, unless I let those fears tell me what to do. I learned that a brave person isn't someone who is fearless, but is someone who overcomes their fears and does something even though they're afraid.

And maybe most importantly, I learned that zombies aren't all *that* scary... though if I don't see one for a long time, that will be okay with me.

The town is coming along very nicely. I think that in a few more weeks we'll be done, and I can start building my castle. Maybe we'll just keep building, and turn this little village into a city.

I keep trying to tell the villagers that I'm just an average guy who has a knack for building, but they still think I'm a hero of some kind. I'm doing my best to not let it go to my head. After all, there are still plenty of things that I'm afraid of. Like spiders. And clowns. And purple foods. And, if I'm being honest, talking to girls my age. (Just don't tell anyone, okay, diary?)

I'm going to keep helping Charlie overcome his fears, and maybe he can help me with a few of mine. Tomorrow we're going to climb the clock tower to try to help him get over his fear of heights. Who knows, maybe some of the villagers will come with us, and we'll help them too while we're at it.

Day 28

Dear Diary,

I know, I know… it's been almost a week since I've written anything, but what a busy week it's been!

New people are coming to our town every day. Most of them are travelers that are looking for a nice place to settle, just like I was. Others are people that came from other cities because they heard about our blossoming village somehow and wanted to see it for themselves. And almost all of them tell me that they saw the huge clock tower and knew they had come to the right place.

Mr. Mayor is a little concerned about how we're going to fit all these new people, but I told him that as long as they keep coming, I'll keep building. Oh, and they have to keep bringing bacon pizzas. (A couple of days ago I tried to get Charlie to eat a pineapple pizza. He still hasn't forgiven me for that one. Let's just say he didn't like it very much.)

Today we had another newcomer. I was working on rebuilding the pizzeria when this person strolled into town, came right up to me and tapped me on the shoulder. I turned to find a girl right around my age with blonde hair and blue eyes.

She smiled and said, "Hi! I'm Felicia. So you're a builder here, huh? I like to build stuff too. Whatcha working on?"

I froze up. I opened my mouth to speak, but no sound came out. Luckily, Charlie stepped in for me.

"This is Minecraft Steve," Charlie said. "And he's very pleased to meet you."

"Oh, *the* Minecraft Steve?" said Felicia. "I heard that you fought off a whole cave of zombies to save your friend! Everyone's talking about it! Is it true?"

"It is true," Charlie said. "In fact, that was just last week, and I was that friend."

"Wow!" said Felicia.

I still couldn't muster a word. I just stood there with my mouth open, trying to think of something to say, but it was like my brain had shut down or something.

Charlie looked me over and laughed a little. "I guess we have some more work to do, huh Steve?"

THE END

Book 2 – Beneath The Surface

Day 163

Dear Diary,

It's me, Steve—or should I say Minecraft Steve, which is what almost everyone calls me these days. Well, except for Felicia and Charlie... but I'll come back to that in a little bit.

You might be wondering, diary, why I started you at Day 163, and not Day 1. That's a weird place to start, right? Well, I have to confess something: You're not my first diary. I had another one before you, but I filled up all the pages, so I had to start a new one. And it just so happens that your first entry is Day 163.

I know what you're wondering next: "Day 163 of what, Steve?" And I'll tell you: It's been 163 days since I came to this place from that *other* place. "This place" was just a tiny village when I first got here, and... Well, I don't really like to talk about that *other* place, so don't bother asking.

Anyway, like I said, this place was just a tiny village when I first arrived, just a bunch of squat, square gray buildings on a big flat plain. Very boring, if you ask me. But the people here were really nice, so I stuck around for a little while.

See, I always wanted to be a great builder, but the place I came from—sheesh, you got me talking about it anyway—let's just say I didn't have a lot of room to be creative. That's all I'm going to write about it. The people in the village never had a real builder, so when I started making stuff, they were amazed. You should have seen the looks on their faces when I built a simple cabin for myself! Soon they had me rebuilding the whole village, which wasn't a problem, because I was doing what I love.

(Then there was this whole big thing with zombies that lived in a cave in the forest nearby, and they kidnapped my friend Charlie, and I had to face my fears and go save him—I'm crazy-scared of zombies—but I wrote all about that in my first diary, so I'm not going to repeat all that here.)

Anyway, it wasn't long before word spread across the land that I was rebuilding this village, and soon a whole lot of new people came to live here. And that's when people started calling me Minecraft Steve (even though if you ask me, I'm still plain ol' Steve). I made a few friends, I get to do what I've always wanted to do, and most importantly, the people here keep me well-supplied with pizza and hot dogs. (The hot dog thing was nearly a disaster; more on that later.)

And if you can believe it, all of that happened in the last 162 days, which is why I'm starting this diary on Day 163, which is today!

So let's see, what happened today? Ah, that's right—I finished my castle! Oh, right, I should probably explain that. See, my dream was always to be a great builder, and part of that dream was that I wanted to build a castle for me to live in. So I did. I've been working on it for the last couple of months, and today I put the last piece in place. It's *very* cool—it's not huge, but it's got two towers, and a drawbridge, and it sits up on a little hill overlooking the city.

Oh yeah, I should probably tell you about that too... the little village I mentioned? It's not really a little village anymore. Now it's more of a small city. See, once the word got out that this village was being rebuilt, all sorts of people came looking for it. They could see it from a mile away because I built a huge red clock tower right in the center of it—so what a lighthouse does for boats, this clock tower did for our village: it brought people in. *Lots* of people... so many people that we didn't honestly know what to do with them all! We had to build all kinds of new houses, so our village got bigger. Then we had to build new shops and stuff for all the new people, so our village got even bigger. Then we had to build new roads, new schools, new parks... I think you get the idea. Before we knew it, our village was no longer a village, but an actual city!

I keep saying "we" because it wasn't just me who did all this. That would have taken a lot more than 163 days! I had help from a lot of people, but two in particular: Charlie and Felicia. They're my two best friends in the whole world, and they help me out a lot. I'd love to go into all the details about them, but it'll have to be another day. I'm exhausted! Tonight is my last night in the cabin, and tomorrow me and Charlie move all our stuff to the castle.

Goodnight, diary!

Day 164

Dear Diary,

Maybe I was a little too quick to move into the castle. I mean, I didn't think it was too big, but after me and Charlie got all our stuff in there, we realized that there was a whole lot of empty room. At first I wasn't sure what to do with all that space, but then I realized I could jazz it up, Minecraft Steve-style! So one room is going to be a trampoline room, where the floor is bouncy and you jump all you want. Another room is going to be the "angry room," so when you're mad about something, you can go in there and shout and yell and stomp around and no one else can hear you. Then there's going to be a ping-pong room that is just one giant ping-pong table! Doesn't that sound awesome?

It didn't sound so awesome to Charlie, because he didn't know what ping-pong is. Sometimes I forget that there are things I know about that the people here don't. Like hot dogs—that's right, thanks for reminding me, diary! I wanted to tell you about the hot dogs.

See, I have two favorite foods: pizza and hot dogs. But the folks here had no idea what a hot dog was! I tried to explain it to them, but the truth is, *I'm* not even sure what's in a hot dog, so I couldn't really describe it. You should have seen the looks on their faces when I even said the words "hot dog." They thought it was food made out of dog! That's why it was nearly a disaster—if I hadn't corrected them, some poor dog might have become someone's dinner! After a lot of trial and error, the city's best cook managed to make something that looked a lot like a hot dog, and *almost* tasted like a hot dog—close enough for me. I'd rather have something that's almost like a hot dog than no hot dogs at all.

Anyway, after I explained what ping-pong is to Charlie, he thought it was great, and wanted to play right away. The problem is, Charlie is a chicken. And I don't mean he's a fraidy-cat—although he is that sometimes—but I mean he's an actual chicken that talks. I know, anywhere else that would seem weird, but here, it doesn't matter much.

Since he's a chicken, Charlie doesn't have fingers, so we had to duct-tape the ping-pong paddle to his wing. Boy, was he bad at it! But I'm sure he'll get the hang of it.

After we moved all of our stuff and figured out what to do with the extra rooms, Felicia came by to check out the castle. I think she was impressed, but she didn't really show it much. She just smiled and said, "I knew you could do it," like I got an A on a quiz or something, instead of building a *whole* castle by myself.

Felicia is definitely the coolest girl I know. She came to the village when it was still a village, only about a month after me. She had heard about my building from a city far away from here, and came all this way just to see what the big deal was. At first she was super impressed, but as we became better friends, she seemed to realize that I'm kind of a goofball.

Honestly, Diary? That's one of my biggest problems—actually, that's one of my *only* problems. Everyone here thinks I'm so great, and stories of our city have reached far and wide, and they call me Minecraft Steve… And then when I saved Charlie from those zombies, man, did that make things worse! After that, everyone thought I was some big hero, *and* a great builder. But really, I'm not anything special. At least I don't think so.

That's why I'm glad to have a couple of good friends that know the real me. I can be myself around them, and they're okay with that. They don't need the big hero builder Minecraft Steve; they just want to hang out with the regular, plain ol' goofy Steve.

Anyway, so Felicia came to the castle and she started looking around, and poking stuff, and generally being her normal, thoughtful self. Felicia is a builder too, like me—well, not quite like me, but she's a builder, and she's pretty good. She has a real eye for color and structure, but if you ask me, she needs some work in the design department—meaning that the things she builds are nice and all, but they're not really eye-catching. (I'm not trying to be mean, but hey, a plain red building isn't much better than a plain gray building, if you ask me.)

After she got done poking around everything, she asked, "So you two are just going to live in a castle now, huh?"

"Yup," I said.

"Like you're king of the city or something?"

I frowned when she said that. I hadn't thought of it that way. A castle does kind of send a weird message, doesn't it? I definitely don't want anyone to think of me as a king of anything—I have enough problems as it is just being Minecraft Steve, without being King Minecraft Steve too.

"Aha!" I said. "I got a great idea." So I made a sign, and in big, sloppy letters, I painted the words "STEVE'S PAD" on it and I hung right outside the drawbridge.

"There," I said. "Now it's not a castle—it's just a pad."

Felicia rolled her eyes when I said that. I don't think she understands how great my solution was.

Day 167

Dear Diary,

I'm bored.

I know I skipped a couple of days of writing in you, which I normally only do when I'm super busy. But I haven't been busy. I just haven't had anything interesting to write about.

The city is built. The castle—I mean, the pad—is finished. There's nothing for me to do right now.

I tried jumping around in the trampoline room for a while, but that was only fun for about an hour. Then I tried playing ping-pong with Charlie, but he's still not very good, so it wasn't very fun to keep winning. I even put on some big heavy boots and stomped around the angry room for a while. I don't know why I thought that would be fun… that's how bored I am!

Felicia is busy building herself a new house on the edge of the city, close to the forest. I offered to help, but she wants to do it by herself, just like I did with the castle—sorry, I meant the pad.

There are plenty of houses and shops to go around, so nobody needs anything built. I guess I could just build something for fun, but if it doesn't have a purpose, if nobody needs it, then what's the point?

I don't know. I guess I'll sleep on it. Maybe something will come to me.

Day 168

Dear Diary,

Something came to me! Okay, I actually shouldn't take all the credit for that. It wasn't really my idea. Let me explain…

This morning I was so bored I decided to play "I Spy" with Charlie. And by "play with Charlie," I mean I followed him around naming things I saw.

"I spy something in this room that's… white," I said.

Charlie sighed. "Is it me?"

"Yes!" I said. "Okay, I spy something in this room that's… yellow."

"Is it my beak?" Charlie said flatly.

"Yes, it is! Okay, I spy—"

"Hey," Charlie interrupted. "Why don't you go see what Felicia is doing?"

I don't think Charlie was really getting into the spirit of the game. So I went for a walk to see how Felicia was doing with her new house. When I arrived, she was working on building the second floor.

"Hey Felicia," I said as cheerfully as I could. "I spy something in this room that's—"

"Let me stop you right there, Steve," she said, and she held a hand up. "You're obviously bored."

"I am," I admitted. "I'm super bored. Can I help you build your house?"

"No way, Jose," she said. (That was a phrase I taught her. She never even heard of the name Jose before that.) "I have to do this on my own. Why don't you go build something somewhere else?"

"Because," I said, "nobody needs anything built right now."

"Then build something for fun," she suggested. Exactly like I thought the night before, right?

"But if nobody needs it, then it has no purpose, so what would be the point?" I said.

She stopped building and thought about this for a whole minute. I knew she was thinking because she sat down on the floor with her legs crossed Indian-style and furrowed her forehead until her eyebrows almost came together.

"Okay…" she said. "You don't want to build unless somebody needs it… and nobody needs anything here… so that means, you need to go somewhere else!"

"Very funny," I said. "You're just trying to get me to go away, aren't you?"

"No, Steve, I mean it." She looked serious. "When you came here, they needed you, right? Now they don't. But somewhere else might need you just like this village needed you."

I thought about that for a moment. It sounded like it made sense. "But that means that I'd have to go away. I like it here. All my stuff is here too, and my cool pad."

Felicia rolled her eyes. "I don't mean go away forever. I just mean go to a new place long enough to help them, and then come back home."

"Home," I said. That sounded good. In all the time I've been here, I hadn't once thought to call it "home," at least not that I could remember. "That's not a bad idea. But how do I find a place like that? I kind of found this village by accident."

Felicia shrugged. "A lot of people have heard of you by now. Maybe we can put the word out that you're willing to help rebuild places that need it."

"Huh." I couldn't deny that it was a good idea. And it would just be for a little while, and then I could come back, relax, do whatever needs doing around here… and then who knows? Maybe go help some other village that needs rebuilding.

"Okay," I said. "Let's put the word out that Minecraft Steve is coming to a village near you!"

Day 169

Dear Diary,

Well, that didn't take long! We just put the word out yesterday, and we've already had three places come to ask for my help. It seems that as soon as folks heard that "the great Minecraft Steve" would travel to other villages, all kinds of places wanted my building skills!

(By the way, diary, it wasn't my idea to call myself "the great" Minecraft Steve… that was Mr. Mayor. Apparently when he sent messengers out, that's what he told them to call me!)

Anyhow, by the very next day, we had three people come to see us. Me, Felicia, Mr. Mayor, and Charlie met with them one at a time in Mr. Mayor's office.

Before the first one came in, I asked Felicia if she would come with me and help. She seemed kind of surprised that I would ask.

"Of course I would," she said. "They can't expect you to rebuild a whole village by yourself!"

I was about to say that, actually, that's exactly what had happened with *this* village, and it was now a small city, but then I remembered that Felicia had arrived just in time to help me, and she had actually helped a lot. So I kept my big mouth shut.

"Hey," Charlie asked, "aren't you going to ask if I'm going to come too?"

I smiled. "Nah, I know you'll come with me. What would you do here all by yourself?"

Charlie just shrugged and continued pecking at the ground. He's so weird sometimes.

The first person that came was a woman with gray hair that said she was the mayor of a little village on the other side of the forest.

"We could really use your help, Minecraft Steve," she said.

"What's wrong with your village?" Felicia asked her.

"Wrong?" the woman seemed confused. "Well, nothing is *wrong* with it… we would just really like some new homes. And some more color. And maybe a nice big clock tower, like you made here."

"I see," Felicia said. It seemed that Felicia wanted to do all the talking. "Well thank you for coming. We'll let you know soon!"

After the woman left, I said, "She seemed very nice. I think we should help her village."

Felicia rolled her eyes. "But Steve, you said you wanted to rebuild places that *need* it. They don't need it; they just want it."

I didn't really see the difference, so I just shrugged as the next person came in. This one was a man, and he wore a nice suit and a tie and shiny shoes. He said that he was a "city planner."

It turned out that he wasn't from a village at all, but from a small city not far away. Again, Felicia asked what was wrong with his city, and he looked just as confused as the woman did.

"Oh, there's nothing wrong with our city," he said proudly. "It's a great place! It's very bright and colorful and filled with nice people. But we'd really like a museum. And a hotel. And maybe a casino. And a zoo, and an amusement park—"

"Okay," Felicia said, interrupting the man. "We get the idea. Thank you for coming, and we'll let you know soon!"

Once he was out the door, I said, "What was wrong with that one?" I really liked the idea of building a zoo or an amusement park.

"Steve, it's the same problem!" Felicia said. "They *want* all those things. If they needed a school, or a library, that would be different."

"Sure," I said, but I wasn't really understanding what she was trying to say. "I get it." (I didn't.)

The third person that came in was just a little girl. She couldn't have been more than 11 or 12 years old. And boy, was she weird looking! Her skin was very, very pale, and her eyes were big and blue. Even her hair was so blonde that it was almost white. I hate to say it, but I thought she was a little bit creepy. She kind of reminded me of a scary movie I'd seen when I was little, with kids that looked like her.

But Felicia smiled at the little girl and said, "What's your name?"

"My name is Agnes," said the little girl. "And I am from a village not far from here. My family doesn't know I came to see you."

"Well, what's wrong with your village, Agnes?" Felicia asked.

"It's not in very good shape," said Agnes. She stared at the floor instead of looking at me or Felicia.

"Some of the houses are falling apart. Walls and roofs crack, and there's no one around to fix them. We don't have a builder, and the people that live in my village don't like to let in strangers."

"That sounds terrible!" Felicia said. "Don't you think so, Steve?"

"Uh, yeah," I said. I was listening—really, I was—but part of me was also thinking about what kind of pen I would build for tigers if I was making a zoo. "Sounds terrible."

Felicia smiled at the little girl and said, "Agnes, we're going to help you rebuild your village."

"Really?" said Agnes, and she smiled wide.

"What?!" I said, maybe a little too loudly.

Day 170 (Day 1 of our trip)

Dear Diary,

I'm not proud of it, but I grumbled a lot today. I grumbled while I packed my bag. I grumbled while we walked out of our little city—me, Felicia, Charlie, and Agnes—and I grumbled as we started on our long hike to Agnes's village.

I grumbled because I wasn't very happy.

Felicia insists that the right thing to do is to help a village that *needs* help, not just one that *wants* help. She said, "A friend in need is a friend indeed."

I argued by saying that I wasn't friends with anyone in Agnes's village. Really, diary, I wanted to build a zoo. Felicia said that after we help Agnes's village, I can go build ten zoos, if I want.

Since when did she become the boss? I don't know how it happened.

We packed up our stuff this morning and had a nice big breakfast, and then we started on our trip—which is why I named this entry "day 1 of our trip." Since I'm going to a new place, I want to make sure that I record everything the right way!

The whole city turned out to say goodbye to us as we left. People lined the streets like the four of us were some kind of tiny parade. They cheered and whistled, waved and shouted, and said things like, "Come back soon!" and "Don't be gone too long, Minecraft Steve!"

You know, I think everyone in our city was really proud of me, that I was going to help some other village the way I helped them. It felt good for people to recognize it, but it also felt kind of bad because if it wasn't for Felicia, I wouldn't have picked Agnes's village.

Charlie was just happy to be along for the trip. He knew that he wasn't going to be much help with building. He keeps calling himself our "moral support," which really means that he thinks he's here to motivate us. So I told him he could be our "cheerleader." That didn't make him very happy.

"I don't wanna be the cheerleader," he whined.

"Okay," I said. "Then how about you can be our mascot? We'll be Team Chicken!"

I laughed, and Agnes laughed, and even Felicia giggled a little bit, but Charlie actually thought I was being serious.

"That could work…" he said thoughtfully.

We walked for what seemed like forever. As it got dark, we decided to set up a camp and finish our hike in the morning, so we set up our little tent and made a fire. As we did, all I could think about was that little Agnes had made this whole hike by herself to our city—and must have been walking very fast to go the whole way in only one day.

"Hey, what's that?" Charlie asked. With one of his wings, he pointed to a structure in the distance. The land was mostly flat, with some rocks here and there. Not too far in the distance, we could see a big structure that looked like a pyramid.

"I don't know," I said. "Looks like someone did a good job building it, though."

"Yeah," Felicia said. "But it's out here in the middle of nowhere. Who would want to build something like that out here?"

It was very weird, but it was also pretty, so we didn't think too much about it.

Now, diary, I have to go, because all four of us are sleeping in the tent and Felicia is telling me to turn the lights out. Tomorrow, we'll be at Agnes's village, and I'll be sure to tell you all about it!

Day 171 (Day 2 of our trip)

Dear Diary,

In my whole life, I've only ever had one day that was stranger than today, and that was the day I first came here from that "other place." I don't think I'll ever have a day weirder than that one, but today was definitely close. Let me start at the beginning…

In the morning, we woke up and packed up our tent and continued our walk. After about an hour or so, we saw another one of those weird, random structures. This time is was a tower, at least four stories tall, pure white and ending in a point. It was very strange, but it was also very nice. I didn't want to admit it, but it was about as nice as anything I would build.

"Very strange," Charlie said. I agreed with him.

We kept going, and it didn't take us very long; it wasn't even noon before we arrived at Agnes's village.

"We're here!" Agnes said with a big smile on her face.

I looked around. "There's nothing here."

Charlie was confused too. "Is it invisible?"

"Don't be silly," Felicia said. "Agnes, are you sure we're here? There's... well, like Steve said, there's nothing here."

It was true. We were standing in the middle of a big, flat, empty land. There were some big rocks here and there, but there were no buildings. There were no people. There was no village.

Agnes smiled even wider and said, "Follow me!"

She walked over to a rock that was twice as big as her...

and then she pushed it aside as if it weighed almost

nothing. It was a fake rock! And when she pushed it aside,

we could see that there was a hole in the ground underneath

it, and a staircase going down into it!

"Your village..." Felicia said. "It's underground?"

"Yup!" Agnes said. "My people don't like to live

above-ground. The sun hurts their eyes. I'm still young, so

it doesn't bother me too much. Come on, I'll show you!"

Agnes started down the stairs and disappeared into

the hole in the ground. I looked at Felicia. She looked at

Charlie. Charlie looked at me.

"I guess we're going underground," Felicia said.

I said, "I just want to remind you that *I* wanted to

build a zoo."

And we went down into the hole.

The stairs were wide and twisty, but solid, and they had a sturdy banister, so it wasn't scary like I expected it to be. We hadn't gone very far when Charlie whistled.

"Wow," he said. "Look at that!"

The stairs led down into a huge underground cavern, big enough to… well, big enough to fit a whole village into, which is exactly what we were looking down at. The streets were all made of smooth gray stone, and little buildings and houses were arranged very neatly in a grid pattern. We could hear the sound of rushing water, so somewhere nearby there had to be an underground river or spring.

The whole thing was very beautiful. It almost didn't seem real.

As we got closer, I could see what Agnes was talking about when she said that their village needed help. There were big cracks running the whole length of some of the streets. The walls and roofs of most of the buildings were cracked too, and some of those cracks had made smaller cracks, like a spider web, reaching out and threatening to collapse the homes.

I didn't get to look too carefully, though, because as soon as we reached the ground of the big cavern, we were suddenly surrounded by people. And not just any people; these people all had the same pale skin and big blue eyes like Agnes.

And they all looked pretty mad.

"Agnes!" scolded an old man with a long white beard. "Why have you brought strangers to our village?"

"They're here to help, Mr. Mayor!" said Agnes. (The old man with the white hair must be their mayor, I guessed.) She pointed at me. "This is the great Minecraft Steve, and he came to help us rebuild!"

"Is that true?" asked the old man, looking at me now. "Did you come to help us?"

"I…" I started to say something, but it kind of got caught in my throat. I was being stared at by a few dozen very pale people with big blue eyes, and most of them still looked angry. I have to admit, it was creeping me out a bit.

"Yes," Felicia said loudly, and she nudged me with her elbow. "We came to help you."

Their white-haired Mr. Mayor stroked his long beard. "I see. Well, we don't normally allow strangers into our village. They usually don't understand our way of life. They think we're creepy and strange."

Boy, you got that right, I thought in my head. But I didn't dare say it out loud.

"If you are really here to help, then I will have to speak with the village council," said their Mr. Mayor. "You may stay here tonight and rest. In the morning, we will let you know if you can stay and help us, or if you will go back where you came from."

They let us stay in a small empty cabin on the outskirts of the village. Right now, as I write this entry, Felicia and Charlie are playing checkers nearby. I honestly can't tell if it's day or night, but I do know that I'm tired from all that hiking. I guess we'll see what the village council says tomorrow, but really, if they don't want us to stay, I think that's okay with me.

Day 172 (Day 3 of our trip... I think)

Dear Diary,

I had to say "day 3 of our trip... I think" because down here in this cavern, I'm really not sure if it's a new day or not. When I woke up, it felt like morning, but there was no sunshine and there were no birds singing. It's weirdly quiet down here, and when there are noises, they echo around the cavern walls. Even though it all looks very pretty, I don't think I like it very much.

Their Mr. Mayor came to our little cabin "in the morning" (at least I have to assume that it was morning, since I couldn't tell) and told us that he had met with the village council, and that if we wanted to stay and help them build, that's okay with them.

He said it very strangely, like it didn't matter at all if we stayed or not. It was weird because Agnes had made it seem like her village *needed* the help, but their Mr. Mayor said it like it was no big deal. I could tell that Felicia thought it was weird too, because her eyebrows furrowed and almost came together like they do when she's thinking hard about something.

"When we were coming down the stairs," she said, "we saw big cracks in the streets and walls and roofs. It looks like you really need to rebuild."

Their Mr. Mayor just shrugged. "They're just cracks," he said simply. "Nothing we can't patch up."

"But what are they from?" Felicia asked him.

"Oh, buildings get old," he said. "You know how it is." He turned toward the door and started to leave. "If you want to stay and help, you can. But if you don't, that's okay too. We'll wait for your answer." And then he left us alone in the cabin.

Once he was gone, Felicia said, "I think we should stay and help them. What do you think, Charlie?"

Charlie shrugged one of his wings. "That sounds okay to me."

"Well, I don't want to," I blurted out.

Felicia looked at me, surprised. "Why not?"

"Because…" I didn't really want to tell her, but I thought I should be honest. So I was. "Because no one will see it."

Felicia blinked a couple of times, like people do when they hear something that they don't understand. "What does that mean?"

"This whole village is underground. No one above-ground will ever see the work we do here," I explained. "We could build the best village ever, and it won't matter."

"Of course it will matter!" she said loudly. "You'll be helping these people!"

"Yeah, about that… don't you think these people are kind of creepy?" I asked sheepishly.

Felicia's mouth kind of fell open, like she was shocked by what I'd said. "Steve! Are you really telling me that you don't want to help these people because of the way they *look*?"

I have to admit, when she said it like that, it really made me feel bad. But it was the truth. That was exactly what I was thinking.

But she wasn't done with me yet.

"So the great Minecraft Steve can't help a poor village in need because no one will see his masterpiece, and besides, the people are weird-looking!" She threw up her hands to show how frustrated she was. "Fine. Then why don't you just leave? Me and Charlie will build this place back up, just the two of us! Right, Charlie?"

Charlie opened his beak to say something, but now I was mad too. Maybe I was being kind of selfish, but now she was trying to take my best friend away! No way that was happening.

"If I leave, Charlie's coming with me!" I shouted.

"Charlie's staying here!" she shouted back.

Charlie just looked from me to Felicia and back to me and then back to Felicia. Finally he opened his beak and went, "SQUAWK!"

We both stopped suddenly. Neither of us had ever heard Charlie squawk before.

"That means 'shut up' in chicken," he said. He looked at me. "Charlie isn't going with you," he said, and then he looked at Felicia and said, "Charlie isn't going with you, either. Charlie is going for a walk by himself. You two need to work this out. Until then, you don't have a mascot!" And then he turned and walked right out of the cabin.

After he was gone, Felicia turned to me and said, "I still think you're being very inconsiderate, but if you want to go, then you can go. I'm staying."

And then she walked out too.

That's when I grabbed you, diary, and wrote all this down. I guess I just needed to vent. I mean, how can Felicia not see things from my point of view? I'm Minecraft Steve. People should see the great things I build. And people should need me to build them.

I don't think I'm being inconsiderate... am I?

Day 172 (Day 3 of our trip – Part 2)

Dear Diary,

It is, after all, daytime. I only know this because I am above-ground again. I'm out in the sunlight, in the warmth, where birds sing and the breeze rustles trees and there are clouds in the sky.

I just don't get it. I don't get how people could live like that, diary.

So I left. Earlier today, after my last entry, I packed up my stuff and I left the little cabin in the big cavern underground. I didn't see Felicia or Charlie, but I didn't look for them either. They will notice, when they get back and I'm not there, that I went back home. Home to my castle… I mean, home to my pad. And my city. And my friends. Well, most of my friends…

As I was leaving the underground village, the little girl Agnes saw me. She ran up to me just as I was about to climb the tall, twisty stairs that led back up to the surface.

"Are you leaving?" she asked, and her voice sounded sad.

"Yes," I said. "I'm leaving. You don't need me here." I left off the part that I didn't want to be there anyway.

"But you can't leave!" Agnes cried. "We do need you here!"

"But your Mr. Mayor sure didn't act like it," I said.

"He doesn't want to admit it, but our village needs help!" She looked like tears were about to start falling.

"Don't cry," I said. "Felicia is staying. She's a good builder. I'm sure she'll help with whatever it is you need." I started up the stairs.

"But…" Agnes started to say.

I stopped. "But what?"

"Nothing," she said quietly.

"Agnes," I asked her, "why does the village stay here? Why not live above-ground?"

"This is our home," she told me. "This is where we've always lived, for my whole life, and my parents' whole life, and even my grandparents' whole life. We don't want to move; we like it down here."

"But it's so great up there!" I said. "There's sunlight and birds and trees and clouds…"

She smiled a little. It looked like a sad smile. "See, you think it's great up there, and we think it's great down here. If I was trying to convince you to live underground, would you?"

"No," I said honestly.

"Right. So why are you trying to convince me that living above-ground is so great?" She turned and sulked away.

She's smart, that Agnes. And she was right; I wouldn't be able to convince the people of her village to just move. So I went up the stairs and back into the glorious sunlight.

I walked for a while. I don't know how long I walked, but based on where the sun was, I guessed that it was sometime in the afternoon. I walked until I saw a long, dark shadow, and I realized that it was that tall, random white tower that we saw when we came here.

I decided to check it out, so I walked right up and I sat in the shadow of it. And that's where I'm writing this entry from, diary. I'm sitting in the big shadow of a totally random white tower in the middle of nowhere. I have no idea who built it, but I'd like to know. It's a very nice tower, with smooth walls, a pointed top, and nice round edges. It's too bad that it's out here in no man's land, where nobody is going to see it...

...

...

Sorry, diary, I didn't mean to get quiet there for so long, but I just had some serious Steve-thinkin' time, and I think I reached an epiphany! (That means "a sudden moment of insight." I know, you're a diary, not a thesaurus.)

See, someone built this beautiful thing out here in nowhere, because they didn't build it for other people...

they built it for themselves. But they probably knew that somebody would see it, and maybe they'd appreciate it.

And then *I* saw it, and *I* appreciated it!

They didn't build this thing for the praise or the reward. They built it because it was what they needed to do at that time. And even though it's out here with nothing around for miles, it still helped somebody... it helped me.

If I ever meet whoever built this strange, wonderful structure, I'm going to shake their hand and make sure that they know they inspired me to do the right thing.

I have to get back and... wait a second, diary, I think I hear someone calling my name.

Yeah, I *do* hear someone calling my name. And there's someone running toward me in the distance. I gotta go! I'll tell you all about it later!

Day 172 (Day 3 of our trip – Part 3!)

Dear Diary,

Who would have thought that so much interesting stuff could happen in one day that it would be enough for *three* diary entries? Yet here we are! I think it's nighttime—yup, I'm back underground—and I'm in the little cabin that their Mr. Mayor let us stay in while we're here.

See, when I was sitting under that big white tower having my epiphany, there *was* someone calling my name, and there *was* someone running toward me. It was Felicia.

By the time she got to me, she was really out of breath. She must have ran all the way from the underground village to the tower.

"You… didn't… leave…. yet," she said. (It was hard for her to talk because she was trying to catch her breath.)

"No, I didn't." I was embarrassed, so I kicked at a stone at my feet. "Actually, I was going to come back."

"Really?" she said.

"Really really. I was just thinking… sometimes I guess we need to do the right thing because it's the right thing to do, and not because someone else is going to see it."

She smiled wider than I'd ever seen her smile before. "Steve, that's the smartest thing you've ever said." Then her smile quickly disappeared. "And I'm glad you're coming back, because there's a real big problem."

"What is it?" I asked her.

"The underground village… it's sinking."

She explained that the whole village was built on the cave floor, which was mostly gray dirt, and not actually solid rock. And the water sound that we heard was an underground river that flowed beneath the city. All that water was making the ground loose, and the whole village was slowly sinking. Every time a house or a street sunk a little further, it would crack the walls they built in their buildings, or the wood in their roofs, or the stones that they used to pave the streets.

"If we don't do something, that whole village is going to fall apart and sink," she said.

"Then what are we waiting for? Let's go!"

We hurried back to the underground village as quickly as we could. Charlie was waiting for us at the bottom of the stairs.

"So?" he asked. "Did you two make up yet?"

"We did," I said. "But now we have work to do."

"Alright! Go Team Chicken!" Charlie said excitedly. "What can I do?"

"You can go tell their Mr. Mayor that we need to have a village council meeting right away," Felicia told him.

And zoom—Charlie was off like a rocket. I'd never seen him move so fast before. I guess feeling like he was really a part of our team inspired him to help out in whatever way he could.

We met with Mr. Mayor and the village council and we told them that we knew what was happening. They admitted that it was true; the village really was sinking!

"Then why not just tell us that?" Felicia asked. "Why would you pretend that you didn't need the help?"

Mr. Mayor said, "Our village isn't used to getting help from strangers. Most people just look at us like we're weird because we like to live underground. I guess we were afraid of telling you that we needed your help."

"Well," I said, "We'll need everyone's help if we're going to save this village."

And we made a plan.

On my way back to the little cabin, I saw Agnes playing hopscotch on a cracked street. She smiled at me and waved. I waved back.

And now, diary, I'm getting some sleep. It's been a really long, weird day, and if our plan is going to work, it's going to take a lot more long, weird days to get it done!

Day 178 (Day 9 of our trip)

Dear Diary,

I know, I haven't been very good about keeping up with my entries, but guess what? I'm busy again! Not only am I busy again, but I'm busier than I've ever been before. Even building our home village into a small city wasn't as hard as this is!

But everyone in the whole underground village has really been pitching in. We started by taking apart the village, section by section. Then, at night (when the sun isn't out) the people of the village have been going above-ground and finding all the big, flat rocks they can find and carrying them back down. We laid a stone foundation

under every building, nice and solid and thick, so that

sinking will never be a problem again. And then we're

rebuilding each house and shop one at a time.

Like I said, it's a lot of work! But you know what? I'm really getting to know the village people here, and they're some of the nicest and hardest-working people I've ever met. I was wrong to judge them because they look weird. Hey, to them, maybe I'm the weird-looking one, right?

I guess I just needed to see things from their point of view. We can't assume that everyone else thinks the same way that we do. If we all thought the same way, the world would be very boring. Everyone would look the same and act the same, and eat the same foods and wear the same clothes.

Being a little different is what makes us all special, I guess.

Anyway, it was another long day (I think) so I'm headed to sleep. Soon we'll be finished, and we can head back home!

Day 185 (Day 16 of our trip)

Dear Diary,

Well, today we wrapped things up. There are a few little things to be done here and there, but the underground villagers told us that they can finish those things up by themselves, no problem. Instead, since it was our last day here, they threw us a huge party, with food and games and music and everything!

Charlie really showed that he was part of the team in another big way. Apparently, he's secretly been teaching the underground village how to make pizza, and for our big going-away party, they brought out several huge bacon pizzas for everyone! It was a great surprise.

At one point during the evening (I think it was evening), Mr. Mayor said he wanted to talk to me and Felicia, so we stepped away from the party for a minute to chat with him.

"I want to say thank you to both of you," he said. "Without your help, our village would have been doomed to sink."

"Aw, shucks, it was nothin'," I said. Felicia elbowed me in the ribs.

"But there's more," said their Mr. Mayor. "You also taught us that we can trust strangers, and that maybe asking for help when we need it isn't such a bad thing."

Felicia smiled and said, "Anytime you need help, you know where to find us."

Diary, I still can't believe we rebuilt that whole village in such a short time. We worked hard, and it wasn't for nothing, because people *will* see it... the people who live here will see it every single day. And you know what else? It's awesome. We did a really nice job—and I don't mean just me and Felicia. I mean the whole village, the way everyone pitched in to help.

And to be honest, I really don't feel like building a zoo anymore. I think I'd rather find other villages that *need* our help, not just the ones that want it.

Before we went to sleep that night, we packed up our stuff so that we could leave first-thing in the morning. As we were packing, there was a knock on our little cabin door. It was Agnes, stopping by to say goodbye.

"Thanks for all your help," she said. "I sure am glad I took the chance to come ask you... and I'm *really* glad that you came to help."

"Yeah, well, I still think living above-ground is way better…" I said, and Felicia elbowed me in the ribs again. (I'm starting to think that's her way of saying, "Shut up, Steve.") I smiled at Agnes to show her I was joking. "It was nice meeting you, Agnes. You should come visit us sometime."

"Maybe I will," she said. "And you could come back anytime, too."

"Maybe we will," we said.

Day 186 (the last day of our trip)

Dear Diary,

So now we get to go home. Me and Charlie can go home to our sweet pad (hey, I didn't say castle that time!) and Felicia can get back to finishing her new house.

I already decided that one of the first things I'm going to do when I get back is talk to our Mr. Mayor and ask him not to call me "the great Minecraft Steve" anymore. They can still call me Minecraft Steve—I like the sound of that—but I don't want people to call me "the great," because honestly, I'm not that great. I'm scared of zombies. I let myself be weirded out by people who were different than me. And I almost walked away from that poor village that needed my help.

But I'm going to try to be better. I'm going to learn from every new lesson, and maybe one day I can be called "great."

Felicia, Charlie and me got up first-thing this morning and set out on our hike back home. We decided to walk faster than we normally would so that we could make the trip in just one day, instead of a day and a half, and that way we wouldn't have to make a camp.

I insisted, however, that we stop briefly at that tall white tower. I just wanted to see it one more time. The three of us stood in the shadow of that big tower and admired it for a few minutes.

I didn't say it out loud, but in my head, I thanked whoever built it. I promised myself that once I got back to our city, I would ask around until I found out who built it, so I could meet them in person. They must be a really good builder—who knows? Maybe even better than me.

As we were standing there, just looking up at the big white tower, Felicia said something really quietly, almost a whisper.

"What was that?" I asked.

"This tower," she said, staring up at it. "It's a giant sundial."

"It's a what?" Charlie asked.

"What time is it?" Felicia asked.

"Uh, I don't know," I said. "Maybe around ten or eleven in the morning?"

"Look!" she said, and she backed up until she was out of the shadow. "That way is north, and the shadow is here… so it's nearly eleven a.m.!" She was really excited now.

And she was right. The tower wasn't just a tower; it was a type of clock that told time based on where the sun was in the sky. How smart is that? Now I *really* needed to find and meet this mysterious builder.

After a little while, we started hiking again, walking twice as fast as normal to make up for the lost time. We walked for hours that way, but it was okay; we were all really happy knowing that we had done a nice thing for that village, and that energy kept us going.

But as we got closer to the city, we started to slow down. We were all exhausted. It was getting too hard to keep that fast pace, so we decided to take a little break, and then finish the last leg of the journey before it got dark.

And that's where we are right now, diary. I'm using our break to jot down the events of this morning and afternoon, because by the time we get back to the city, I'll probably be too tired to hold a pen.

Charlie is up in a nearby tree, shouting that he can see our clock tower from here. He sound excited.

Hang on a second, diary, he's shouting something else now.   ..

I think he just said he sees smoke coming from the city. That doesn't sound good. Is our city in trouble? I have to go, diary. I'll be sure to come back though!

THE END (FOR NOW)

Book 3 – Creeper Catastrophe

Day 186

Dear Diary,

Where I come from, there's a saying that goes, "Where there's smoke, there's fire." Me, Charlie and Felicia were sitting on a hilltop, taking a rest from our long journey when we saw smoke rising up from our little city. So we ran.

I wasn't thinking about the damage to all the things I'd built. I wasn't thinking about all my cool stuff burning up. I was thinking about the people in the city that we had come to call our friends and neighbors, and that they might be in trouble and need our help. I could tell by the looks on my best friends' faces as they ran beside me that they were thinking the same thing too.

(Okay, I have to admit, I was also thinking, *Boy, I sure hope the pizzeria didn't catch fire.* I was really looking forward to a bacon pizza when we got home.)

It felt like it took a really long time to get there. All the worry in my head made my legs feel like they were moving in slow motion, like no matter how fast I ran, it wouldn't be fast enough. Charlie fell behind, because Charlie is a chicken and has little chicken legs and tiny chicken feet. Felicia is fast, though—she kept up with me the whole time, and neither of us took our eyes off the city in the distance as three trails of smoke curled up into the sky from different parts of town. I didn't see any fire, but it was daytime, and it would be hard to see the orange glow in the sunlight, but still, that made me feel a little bit better.

Hang on, diary, let me pause a moment here and take a *big* step back, because you're probably a little confused. See, you're not my first diary. You're not my second diary, either. You're my third diary, which is why this one started on "day 186." That means it's been 186 days since I came here, looking for adventure and a place to build.

My first diary got all filled up. In it, I told the story about how I came to this tiny village that desperately needed a builder. I always wanted to build, so I helped them out. See, all their houses and shops and buildings were these one-story gray cubes. There was no color, no pizzazz (that's a fun word for "something exciting or interesting"), just these boring gray squares. So I helped them out. I built them a tall, red clock tower right in the center of town, and then I built streets, and new houses, and a library, and a new school… almost everything.

I say "almost" everything because after a while, people started coming to our little village—which by then was a town—and one of them was my now-best-friend Felicia. She's a builder too, and together we finished the town. But we didn't stop there. We built and built until we could call it a small city. Even more people came, and now our city is a bright, beautiful place where lots of people work, live and play together. We're really proud of everything we've done.

(There was also this whole thing with zombies that tried to take my friend Charlie and force him to be a horsey for their zombie babies to ride around, but I'm way too tired to go into all that again. It's all in my first diary, and anyone who wants to read it can.)

Right, I totally skipped over Charlie! He was the first friend I made. Charlie the Chicken is, well, a chicken. Actually, he's a *talking* chicken, which would be weird to a lot of people where I come from, but here it's pretty normal. At least no one seems to care much. Charlie is a chicken—meaning that he's a white flightless bird—but he's also a chicken—meaning that he's scared of almost everything. At least he was when I first met him. Charlie has come a long way since then. I helped him get over a lot of his fears, and you know what? He helped me get over a few of mine. Now every time we have an adventure, Charlie is right there beside me. (Except when we were running to the city; his little chicken feet couldn't keep up, so he was behind me, instead of beside me.)

Anyway, after we built up the city, we put the word out that we—me, Felicia, and Charlie—would travel to other places and help them out too. That was all in my second diary, which, sadly, didn't get filled up; it got burned up. But I'll get to that.

A distant village asked for our help, and we agreed. But it turned out that the village was underground, and was slowly sinking further and further down into the soft ground. At first I didn't want to help them out, because they were underground, and who would see it? I wanted people to be able to come and see everything that I built. Me and Felicia argued, and—long story short—I realized that I had to do the right thing because it was the right thing to do, and not because people would praise me for the work I did.

The village was more than a day away, walking like we were, so it took a long time to get back to our city, and when we finally saw it in the distance, there was smoke rising from it. That pretty much catches you up to today, diary. I hope you're less confused now.

So getting back to where I left off, the three of us ran toward the city as fast as our legs would carry us. As we got closer, we heard a noise. Well, we didn't just hear it. We *felt* it too. It was the loudest BOOM! I'd ever heard. It shook the ground under our feet.

I looked at Felicia, and she looked at me. She looked worried. I probably did too. We both had a good idea of what was going on, but neither of us said it.

We finally made our way into the city. The streets were insane. People ran this way and that, some shouting, some crying. Everyone looked scared. Eventually we found the person we were looking for. Mr. Mayor stood in the middle of our main street, near the clock tower. He had both hands on his gray-haired head, and he was looking around with an expression on his face like he couldn't believe what was happening. His gray beard was sticking out in every direction.

I ran right up to him and shook his shoulders. "Mr. Mayor!" I shouted. "What's going on?"

"Oh, Minecraft Steve," he said. "It's terrible! Creepers! Creepers in the city!"

That's what I had thought, and that's what Felicia had thought too. "Is everyone okay?" I asked him.

"Yes, no one is hurt, but everyone else is scared!" Mr. Mayor said "everyone else" like he wasn't scared, even though he certainly looked like it. "What are we going to do?"

The truth is, I didn't know what to do. I had dealt with Creepers before, and the only way I knew how to avoid them was to run away, or to have an ocelot chase them off. Suddenly I remembered... we had an ocelot!

"Mr. Mayor, what about the ocelot? Did you let it out?"

He nodded frantically. "We did! Of course! But there were just too many!"

Too many? I didn't like the sound of that. Felicia took Mr. Mayor by the arm and sat him down on a wooden bench. "Mr. Mayor," she asked him, "how many Creepers were there?"

He shook his head and stared at the ground like he was thinking. "Ten, I think? Maybe twelve?"

I gulped. Twelve Creepers. Yikes. That was way too many for one ocelot to chase away.

"Okay, listen up," I said to everyone. "Me and Charlie will search the city and make sure all the Creepers are gone. Mr. Mayor, you and Felicia will gather everyone up, and we'll have a town meeting to talk about what happened."

"Sounds like a plan," Felicia said.

"Got it," Mr. Mayor agreed.

"Wait, why do *I* have to go on Creeper patrol?" Charlie protested. He was frightened by Creepers. I couldn't blame him; just about everyone was scared of Creepers. But I wasn't.

Me and Charlie checked every street, every house, every alley, and every shop for Creepers. We told every person we passed that there was going to be a meeting right away, and they should all go to City Hall.

It took us a while to search everything, but we didn't see a single Creeper. Charlie, of course, was relieved.

"I want to look at one more place," I said. See, after me and Felicia finished building the city, I was finally able to make my dream come true and build my very own castle. It's really awesome, and Charlie lives there with me. But I didn't want to call it a castle, because that makes me sound like a king or something, so instead, I just call it "my pad." And I know it was a little selfish, but since I knew everyone was okay, and there were no more Creepers in sight, I really wanted to make sure that my pad was okay, too. I worked really hard on it.

So me and Charlie headed up the hill toward our pad.

Sorry, diary, but my hand is cramping up from all this writing. I have to take a break, and I'll come back and tell you the rest of the story in just a little while.

Day 186 (part 2)

Dear Diary,

Much better! So much stuff happened in just this one day that I had to take a little rest before I tell you about the rest. And just so you don't worry too much, I'm writing this from inside my cool pad, safe and sound... mostly.

As I was saying, me and Charlie hurried up the hill to our pad. Did I mention how cool it is? It's got tall gray stone walls, and towers, and a curtain (on a castle, that's the outside stone wall that protects the inside of the castle. Like I said, it's awesome).

It didn't look like there was any damage to the outside of it, but just to be sure, me and Charlie walked around the whole outside of it, checking everything to make sure that nothing got in—and by "nothing" we mean Creepers.

"Looks okay," said Charlie.

"Yeah, it looks just fine—" I stopped before I could finish my sentence, because right as I started talking, I heard a sound. It sounded like air escaping from a flat tire, or maybe a tea kettle right before it starts to whistle.

It sounded like this: *HISSSSSSSSSSSSSSSSSS*...

And I forgot to breathe for a few seconds, because I knew what that sound was.

Me and Charlie, we turned around at the same time, and sure enough, there was a Creeper only a few feet behind us. See, when a Creeper starts hissing, you've only got a couple of seconds to get as far away as you can before it explodes. That was the big BOOM sound we heard earlier, and also the source of the smoke. I think just about everyone knows it, but Creepers dislike people so much that when they get close to them, they blow up.

I didn't even have time to think. I reached down and scooped Charlie up into my arms. Some instinctual part of my brain—that means something you don't learn or think about, you just know it—realized that Charlie wasn't fast enough to outrun the Creeper. So I grabbed him up and I ran.

The BOOM! of the Creeper exploding was so loud that I couldn't hear anything else. It was so mighty that it pushed me forward and I fell flat on top of Charlie. I got up slowly. All I could hear was a ringing in my ears. Charlie got up too. I'm glad he wasn't hurt when I fell on top of him; I'm a lot bigger than he is. But he seemed okay.

The Creeper was gone. In its place was a huge black crater, still smoking from the explosion. And the curtain wall of my castle was destroyed. Where it once stood was just a pile of broken stones.

So much for my awesome pad being okay. But at least *we* were okay, and that's a lot more important than some dumb wall.

When I could finally hear again, I asked Charlie, "Are you okay?"

"Yeah," he said. "But the castle wall is destroyed!"

"It's okay. We'll fix it," I promised him.

"Uh-oh," he said. "That's not all. It looks like your backpack took some damage."

I had been wearing my backpack the whole time, since we got back from the other village, and honestly, I had forgotten all about it. Charlie was right; the force of the Creeper's explosion had torn my backpack open, and all the stuff had spilled out onto the ground. There was only one thing I really cared about though.

My diary, the one I was writing in before I started this new diary, was burned up. Not completely; I could still read most of what I had written, but the cover was torn off, and the edges of all the pages were charred. (And that's why I started you, new diary. I wouldn't have been able to keep writing in that one.)

Charlie patted my back with one of his wings. "Hey, I'm sorry, pal," he said.

I just shrugged. "It's okay." Even though that's what I said, it wasn't what I was thinking. I was thinking, *Stupid Creepers. Why did you have to come here, of all places? Why do you have to blow stuff up? Better yet, why can't you blow up your own stuff?*

Charlie said, "We should really get to that town meeting."

Suddenly I felt very tired. We'd been walking the whole day, and then we came back to the city to find it being blown up by Creepers, and now my diary, and part of my castle, were destroyed. I didn't feel like going to a town meeting. I didn't feel like doing anything at all.

"I don't think I feel like going," I said. "Why don't you go, and tell everyone that there are no more Creepers in the city, and then come back later and tell me what Mr. Mayor said."

Charlie frowned. (Well, Charlie has a beak, so he doesn't actually frown, but I could tell by his eyes that the look he was giving me would be a frown, if he had lips.) "But people will want to hear from you. You're Minecraft Steve. Everyone here listens to you."

"Well, maybe I don't want them to!" I didn't mean to shout, but it came out much louder than I intended. I wasn't mad at Charlie; I was mad at the situation. But still, why does everyone have to look to me for answers? I'm not Mr. Mayor. I'm just Steve.

Charlie looked hurt that I had yelled at him. "Okay, Steve," he said quietly. "I'll go." And he walked off down the hill toward the center of town.

I felt really bad, and I wanted to tell him I was sorry, but I just stood there and watched him go. And then I stared at the blown-up wall for a while. I probably could have rebuilt it right then and there, and it probably wouldn't take me very long, but I didn't feel like it.

Instead I went inside my pad, and I went to my bedroom, and I found you—a new diary. I always keep a couple spare diaries, just in case something happens to one (you know, like if it gets blown up by a stupid Creeper or something).

And then I wrote this. And now I'm exhausted. It's still daylight out, but I don't care. I'm going to sleep.

Day 187

Dear Diary,

A good night's sleep was exactly what I needed! When I woke up this morning, I felt great, recharged, and ready to meet this Creeper problem head-on.

But the first thing I needed to do was apologize to Charlie for the way I acted.

I went out into the courtyard of the castle, where I had built Charlie a chicken coop. It was like his own little mini-pad. I knocked twice on the side of it. A moment later, Charlie stuck his white head out of the small square door.

"Hey, Charlie," I said sheepishly. "Sorry about the way I acted yesterday. I wasn't mad at you; I was mad about that other stuff."

"I know," he said brightly. "No sweat. Sometimes we just need a little time to ourselves to cool down."

I smiled at him. What a great friend, right?

"So, what happened at the town meeting yesterday?" I asked him.

"You should probably talk to Felicia. She's better at explaining that kind of stuff than I am."

"Okay, I'll go see her. You want to come with me?"

Charlie scooted out of the little square door and stretched his wings. "Sure, let's go."

We didn't even use the castle doors; we just walked right out of the big hole in the castle wall. I couldn't help but giggle about it. Who needs a door when you've got a hole, right?

Felicia had started to build a nice house for herself before we left for the underground village. It was on the edge of town, not far from my pad, so it was an easy walk. Her house wasn't quite finished yet, but it was almost done, and lucky for her, the Creepers had left it alone.

When we got there, she was standing outside the front door like she was expecting us. Her arms were folded across her chest and she was tapping one foot.

"Well, well," she said. "Look who decided to show up." I would have thought that she was angry with me, except she was having a hard time keeping the smirk off her face.

"Yeah, sorry," I said. "Some stuff happened, and I just felt like being alone for a bit."

"Charlie told me." She stopped tapping her foot. "Sorry about your castle wall."

I shrugged. "No big deal. Anyway, what happened at the town meeting?"

"I think you should hear it from Mr. Mayor," she said. I rolled my eyes. Wasn't *anyone* going to tell me what was going on?

A few minutes later, me, Felicia, and Charlie were all sitting in chairs around Mr. Mayor's big desk in his office at City Hall. He seemed calmer than he was the day before—but not by much. He still seemed very nervous, and kept looking out his window, where he could see the big red clock tower.

"The people are scared, Minecraft Steve," he said. "And they should be."

That's another thing I should tell you, diary. See, my friends call me Steve. But everyone else, including Mr. Mayor, calls me Minecraft Steve. It started because I'm so fast at building, but it became more than that—after I saved Charlie from the zombies (which wasn't really "saving him" as much as it was "talking with the zombies and coming to an agreement"), everyone started treating me like I was a superhero or something. And then rumors started spreading, even beyond our city, and people from all over the place heard about "the great Minecraft Steve," who fought off a horde of zombies, and rebuilt a whole city in a day—neither of which actually happened. That's the way rumors work, I guess. It all bugs me, especially because at one time, I let the fame get to my head. (That's all in my second diary.) That's why I'm so grateful for my friends. They keep me down to earth, and around them, I can be plain ol' Steve.

Anyway, Mr. Mayor kept looking out the window like he was watching for something, and he kept talking. "The Creepers caused a lot of damage. Thankfully, no one was hurt."

"I guess we're lucky for that," I said.

"That's the weird thing," Mr. Mayor said. "They don't seem like they want to hurt anyone; they seem to just want to destroy our buildings and streets. It's all very strange."

"And that's not even the strangest part," Felicia said.

I squirmed in my seat. "What?"

"Yesterday was not the first time the Creepers have come into the city. It's the third time. It happened two other times while you were away, helping to rebuild that other village."

I jumped to my feet. "Two other times?!" I practically shouted.

"Each time," Mr. Mayor went on, "there were a lot of them, at least ten. They split up and go in different directions, and eventually they explode, and they destroy some part of the town when they do."

"Where are they all coming from?" I had heard of one or two Creepers at a time wandering into a place—it had happened once before when we were still just a little village—but never ten. That was crazy!

Mr. Mayor shrugged. "We don't know. But we do know we need to keep them out. Do you have any ideas?"

I put on my thinking cap—not literally, of course. That just means I thought really hard about it. "We could get some more ocelots," I said. "They're good at chasing Creepers away."

Mr. Mayor shook his head. "It was hard enough just to get one. I have no idea how we would get nine more."

"What about a golem?" Felicia said. "To patrol the city."

"Hey, that's a good idea," I chimed in. Golems are great for getting rid of hostile mobs.

Mr. Mayor shook his head again. "There are just too many of them for one golem," he said. I frowned. I decided that I still wanted a golem.

Finally, Charlie spoke up. "How about a wall?"

"Huh?" we all said at once.

"A wall around the city," Charlie explained.

"I don't think that will work, Charlie," I said. I didn't want to hurt his feelings, but I didn't think it was a very good idea. "You saw what that one Creeper did to our castle wall."

"But we could make it out of oak trees," he replied.

"Stone is stronger than wood," I said back.

"No, wait, Charlie might be right," Felicia cut in. "Stone *is* stronger than wood, but the oak trees in the forest are really thick and strong. With stone, you have to pile a lot of them on top of each other, so the spaces between the stones make weak points. We could use whole tree trunks to build our wall, and it'll be really strong—and thicker than the stone would be."

I thought about it for a long moment. Then I smiled and patted Charlie on the back. "I think it's a great idea," I said. And then I added, "But I still want a golem."

Felicia grinned and rolled her eyes. "Fine, how about this: I'll build you a golem, and you go cut down some oak trees for our wall. Charlie, you should get up in the clock tower and keep a lookout for any more Creepers. If you see any, I want you to squawk twice."

"Aye aye, Captain," said Charlie.

It was a good plan. Charlie's squawk is super loud, and Felicia is going to build me a golem. And all I have to do is cut down some trees. Piece of cake, right? Looks like tomorrow I'll be chopping wood!

Day 188

Dear Diary,

Boy, was I wrong. Felicia's plan was *not* good... at least, not good for me. I've never been so sore in my whole life. Chopping down trees is way harder than I thought it would be. And oak trees are very thick and strong, just like Felicia said.

Spoiler alert: I didn't even get one single tree. But diary, there's a good reason for that!

This morning, Charlie climbed up into the clock tower like he was supposed to. (He used to be afraid of heights, but I helped him get over his fear by going up to the top of the tower with him a bunch of times. Now he can go up there by himself, no problem.)

Felicia started building my golem, as she promised. She's going to make me an iron golem, which is awesome—way better than a snow golem, in my humble opinion.

And me? I grabbed an ax and I headed out to the forest. It's a really big forest, and when I first got here, it was pretty far from the edge of the village, but as we built more and grew into a city, we kept moving the edge of town out further and further until now it almost touches the tree line. So when I say "I headed out to the forest," really I just kept walking until there were trees instead of buildings.

It was in this very same forest that I encountered the zombies that had taken Charlie hostage. See, there's a big cave hidden deep in the woods, and that's where the zombies lived. I have no idea if they're still there or not, and I really didn't want to take any chances. Just to be safe, I brought a bow and arrow with me, in addition to my ax. (I don't actually want to shoot anything; it's more to threaten anything that might get too close, like zombies or Creepers. I'm a pretty good shot, so I was sure I could make it look like I was aiming for them, and then just shoot an arrow real close.)

I decided I would start by finding the biggest, mightiest oak tree I could find and cut it down. That way, every other tree would be easier, right? The plan was that after I was done cutting down the trees, the villagers would all come out to the woods with ropes, and together we would haul the big tree trunks back to make our wall.

Well, diary, I found a great big oak tree. It was so tall that if I stood right next to it and looked straight up, I still couldn't see the top of it. If I put my arms around the massive trunk, my fingers couldn't touch each other on the other side. It was big.

I started chopping. The sound of the ax hitting the wood didn't make a *chop, chop* sound like I expected; instead it sounded like *tock, tock, tock*. After twenty swings, I took a look at my progress. I was already out of breath and my hands kind of hurt from the force of the ax hitting the solid wood.

And I had barely made a dent in the tree. Sheesh! This one tree was going to take me all day!

But I kept at it. A few minutes later I was sweating, and already tired, and there was *still* just barely a cut in the trunk of the tree. I would have given my left arm for a chainsaw!

All through the afternoon I kept chopping at this one tree, taking breaks when my arms got too tired to keep swinging. After a little rest, I would stand up, more determined than ever, and keep on swinging that ax.

While I chopped, my mind wandered. I thought about the zombies in the cave, and I hoped that they weren't still there. I thought about the people in the underground village, and I hoped that they were doing okay. Then I remembered the tall white tower that I had seen on the journey from my city to the underground village.

See, diary, when we made the day-long trip to help that other village, we came across a couple of weird things—like a pyramid right out in the middle of nowhere, and then later, this tall white tower with no doors or windows. Felicia later figured out that the tall tower was a giant sundial, a way of telling time based on where the sun is in the sky.

This is all in my second diary, but the short version is, that random white tower out in the middle of nowhere is what inspired me to help those underground villagers rebuild. I had promised myself that when I got back to our city, I would find out who made it, and try to meet them in person.

The thing is, with all this craziness with the Creepers, I had forgotten all about that. I promise myself, right here and now as I write this, that I *will* find out who built that tower, and thank them personally for motivating me to do the right thing!

Anyway, back to my story: I was so concentrated on chopping down this mighty oak tree and thinking about that white tower that I didn't even notice the Creeper until it was almost right next to me.

Yeah, diary, you read that correctly: a Creeper came up and stood *right next to me!*

I jumped—because it startled me. Certainly not because I was scared of it. No, sir. I dropped my ax to the ground, and at the same time, I snatched up my bow and arrow.

I took a couple of steps back and I said, real loud, "Stop right there!"

"No, it's okay!" said this Creeper. "I'm friendly!"

Now, diary, I have to admit, that was weird. I mean, I guess I assumed that Creepers could talk—after all, one of my best friends is a chicken, and he can talk—but none of them had ever talked to me before. They usually just hissed or exploded.

I stared at this little Creeper. I say "little" because he was actually very small, barely bigger than half the size of an ordinary Creeper. He looked like a Creeper in every other way—he was green, he had black eyes, four legs, and his mouth turned down on both sides like he was always frowning—except for how small he was.

But… a friendly Creeper? Yeah, right.

"Nice try," I said. "The last time I saw a Creeper, it blew a hole in the side of my house! You can't trick me." I notched an arrow on the string of the bow, pulled back, and shot.

Like I said earlier, I don't actually want to shoot anything; I just wanted to scare him away. So I made sure I missed. The arrow sailed just a few inches above his head in a *whoosh*. I notched another arrow so that the Creeper knew I meant business.

And then the weirdest thing happened. The Creeper *hid*. I mean, it didn't run away, and it didn't run toward me—instead he hid behind a tree!

"Please don't shoot me!" he cried out.

I just stood there like a statue, thinking. Creepers don't hide. There was something odd about this little Creeper.

"Why are you hiding?" I called out to him.

"You just shot an arrow at me!" he shouted back.

"Yeah, but... I've never seen a Creeper hide before. Usually they just run at me, hissing, and then..." I trailed off and lowered the bow. I decided that something was *definitely* different about this Creeper, and I was curious. "Hey, come out here. I'm not going to shoot you."

The little Creeper peeked out from behind his hiding tree. He saw that I had dropped the bow, but he still came out slowly, and I swear... he was trembling, like he was really afraid of me.

"You're an odd Creeper," I said, and I took a step toward him. As soon as I did, tall shapes moved in the trees behind the little one. Before I knew it, four full-sized Creepers came out of the brush. I leaped back.

All four of them were hissing. That wasn't good.

"I wasn't going to hurt him!" I said loudly. It didn't matter; the Creepers kept moving forward, getting closer. If I didn't move, they would be close enough to explode in just a second or two. So I grabbed up my ax, my bow, and my arrows, and I ran away.

See? There's just no reasoning with Creepers... well, except maybe one.

Day 189

Dear Diary,

Today I met with Felicia, Charlie, and Mr. Mayor again, to tell them the bad news: Our plan wasn't going to work. It was just too much trouble to cut down enough oak trees to build a giant wall. It would take everyone in the whole city with hundreds of axes to chop down that many trees!

Besides, there was another thing that we hadn't thought of before. To cut down that many trees would mean practically destroying the forest, and none of us wanted to do that. Birds and squirrels and all sorts of other animals lived there.

Everyone agreed with me, but they agreed sadly, because it meant we were back to square one—which means that we had to make a new plan from the beginning.

At least that's what they thought. See, diary, I already had a new plan, but I couldn't really tell them that. Why, you might ask? Well, because they would think I was crazy.

"I think the Creepers are coming from somewhere in the forest," I told them all.

"What makes you say that?" Felicia asked me.

"Because when I was chopping down a tree yesterday, four of them came out of the woods, hissing."

Charlie gasped. "You must have barely escaped!"

I nodded. "That's why I think I should go back into the woods and find out where they're living."

Mr. Mayor's mouth dropped open. "You want to *find* the Creepers?"

"Yes," I said. "Maybe I can talk to them, get them to stop coming into our city."

"You can't reason with Creepers!" Mr. Mayor almost shouted.

"Do you have any other ideas?" I asked. No one said anything, so I kept talking. "Charlie, you stay up in the clock tower and keep an eye out for Creepers. Felicia, you should start rebuilding what the Creepers already destroyed. And me, I'll go into the woods and try to find them."

Diary, you're probably wondering two things: First, why I didn't tell them about the little Creeper that I talked to, and second, why I would try something so crazy like attempting to reason with the Creepers. See, that's my secret plan: I want to find that little Creeper again. He seemed reasonable, and maybe even friendly, like he said, so I want to seek him out and talk to him. Then maybe he can talk to the other Creepers for me, and together, we can come up with a solution.

I knew that if I told the others about my plan they would think I was more nuts than they already thought I was. I mean, whoever heard of a friendly Creeper, right? Before yesterday, I wouldn't have thought that it was possible.

Anyway, the others agreed with me, and made me promise that I would be extra-super-careful going into the woods by myself. Felicia really wanted to come with me, but I told her it was way too dangerous. After our meeting was over, though, I pulled Felicia aside and asked her for a special favor.

"Sure, Steve," she said. "Whatever you need."

"Do you remember that tall white tower we saw on the way to the underground village?" I asked her.

"Of course, the big sundial. What about it?"

"Do you think you could ask around and see if anyone knows who built it?" I didn't want to forget the promise I had made to myself.

Felicia looked confused, but she nodded. "Sure, Steve. I'll ask around."

"Great, you're the best." She smiled and told me again to be careful.

I decided I would wait until tomorrow to go into the woods, start fresh in the morning. I headed back to my pad and waved hello to Golem.

Oh, right, I forgot to tell you, diary; Felicia finished my iron golem. I decided to call him Burt. I didn't really have a reason for calling him that, other than that I liked it. (It's also nicer than calling him "Golem".) He moves kind of slow, but he patrols the outside of the castle, keeping it safe from intruders. He's a pretty swell guy.

"Hey, Burt," I said. "Anything new?"

"Not much," he said. "Oh, wait. There was a Creeper here to see you earlier."

"*What?*" I said loudly. "A Creeper was here? Did you fight him off?"

"Well, no," said Burt. "He just wanted to… talk."

"A Creeper wanted to talk." I couldn't believe my ears. "Wait a second! Was he real little?"

"They're all little to me," said Burt. He had a good point; he was so tall that everyone was shorter than him.

"I mean, was he smaller than an average Creeper?"

Burt thought for a moment. "Yeah, I guess he was. But it doesn't matter now. I told him to buzz off."

Argh! I was so frustrated. See, I couldn't tell Burt that what he did was wrong; his job is to keep my pad safe, so technically, he did the right thing. But at the same time, he shooed away the only Creeper I actually *wanted* to see!

"Listen, Burt. If that same Creeper comes back, let him in. He's okay. But he's the only one, okay?"

Burt frowned. "Well, okay. What are you going to do?"

"I'm going to try to find him."

Burt shrugged. "You're the boss." He lumbered away, back on his patrol, and I swear as he did I heard him mutter, "People are weird."

Day 190

Dear Diary,

Here I am, back in the woods again. It seems like it wasn't that long ago that I was searching these same woods for the source of zombies, and now here I am searching for Creepers! That's me, Minecraft Steve, always running headfirst into danger.

I must be crazy, right?

This morning I got up early and packed a backpack (a new one, not my old burnt-up one) full of some stuff I'd need, just in case it takes me a while to find them. I packed some extra clothes, a rope, a pickax, my bow and arrows, a blanket, and a bunch of apples for snacking, and I headed into the woods, alone, the find wherever the Creepers were calling home.

I figured the best place to start would be the old zombie cave. I *really* didn't want to go there, especially not by myself, but it made the most sense—I've been inside the cave before, so I know it's much bigger on the inside than it looks from the outside. It would be the perfect place for so many Creepers to be living.

It wasn't hard for me to find it again. Once I did, I hid behind a big tree far enough away from the entrance so that I could see it, but no one could see me. I watched the mouth of the cave for a long time. I don't know how long I stood there, hidden behind the tree with just a small part of my head poking out so that I could see, but it must have been at least an hour. In that whole time, I didn't see anything—no movement, no patrol, and most importantly, no zombies.

Eventually I gathered my courage and I carefully made my way to the cave's entrance. I peeked inside. My whole body was tense. I was ready to run away if I needed to. But it turns out I didn't have to run, because there wasn't anyone—or anything—in the cave. It looked like the zombies had moved out. I wonder where they went. Maybe they found a new cave. Or maybe they left the woods entirely. (That would make me feel much better at night!)

Anyway, after I checked the cave, I continued up the sloping hillside so that I had a good vantage point—that means a good place to see from. The hill wasn't big enough to see over the tops of the trees, but I could still see a lot of the forest in every direction. But I didn't see any Creepers. Not a single one!

Since then, I've been wandering around the woods just looking. I have no idea where else to go or what else to look for. As it started to get dark, I climbed up a big tree and tied myself to a thick limb so I wouldn't fall out, and then I took out my blanket and wrapped it around myself. I'll sleep here in the tree tonight, diary. Tomorrow—I'm going to find those Creepers!

Day 191

Dear Diary,

I didn't find those Creepers. I spent the whole day roaming around these woods and didn't spot anything out of the ordinary. Tomorrow's another day, I guess.

Day 192

Dear Diary,

Where I come from, there's another saying that goes, "Even smart people can lack common sense." That means that it doesn't matter how much you know, or how well you do in school; sometimes people just don't think about the most obvious answer to a problem. Let me explain:

I spent half the day searching the woods again. At some point in the afternoon, I kind of gave up. I just sat down on a big moss-covered stone and stayed there for a while. As I was sitting there, thinking about going back home, I heard a noise, like a rustling in a nearby bush. I jumped up and reached into my backpack for my bow and arrows, but before I could get them out, three pigs came into the clearing.

There were two very large pigs—easily as big as me—and an adorable little piglet between them. I must have looked frantic, or maybe frightened, with my hands halfway inside my backpack, because the father pig chuckled and said, "So sorry! We didn't mean to scare you."

"Uh… it's okay," I said. I'd never spoken to a pig before. But then again, I talk to a chicken every day, and a few days ago I had a conversation with a Creeper, so why not a pig?

The three pigs walked through the clearing and were about to leave when the mama pig turned to me and said, "Are you lost?"

"No, not lost," I replied. I knew my way back home, but that's not what I was here for, you know. "I'm actually looking for something. Say… you wouldn't happen to know where the Creepers live, do you?"

"Oh," said the mama pig. "You mean the Valley of the Creepers. Sure, we know where it is. Actually, you're not very far from it right now."

And that's where I lacked common sense—I suddenly realized that at any point in the last two days, instead of wandering around the woods, I could have just stopped and asked any of the animals for help! (Duh, Steve!)

The father pig gave me directions on how to get there, and mama pig was right—I was no more than a ten-minute hike from the quarry where the Creepers lived.

"But why would you want to go there?" the father pig asked. "That's where they raise little Creepers into big Creepers."

Aha! I thought to myself. So *that* was why the Creepers were only destroying buildings, and not hurting anyone—they were training new Creepers!

I quickly explained my problem to the pigs. I told them about our city, and about how the Creepers were using our buildings to teach them how to explode properly. I even told them about the friendly Creeper, and how I hoped that talking to him could help us all.

"Friendly Creeper?" the little piglet finally spoke, in a tiny, squeaky voice. "Why, I know him! He helped me find my parents again when I was lost."

So he *was* really a friendly Creeper. My heart leapt with joy. There was a chance my plan would work!

"Thank you for the directions!" I said, and I hurried along. Those pigs were so nice that I suddenly felt *really* bad about all the bacon pizza I've eaten.

Anyway, the Valley of the Creepers turned out not to be a real valley, but a rock quarry where miners had once dug for stone. And it was filled—and I mean *filled*—with Creepers.

I heard them before I saw them. As I got closer, I heard a number of booms coming from nearby. Some were small, little booms, and others were very loud, thunderous booms. I guessed that this was where they taught Creepers how to explode, and then they were bringing them to our city to practice destroying things! It made me so angry that I didn't even try to hide. I marched right up the edge of that quarry so that I was looking down at the sea of Creepers.

One of them saw me almost right away, and he shouted out, "Hey! Intruder!"

Suddenly every Creeper was looking up at me, hundreds of eyes staring. The big creeper who had shouted at me asked, "Who goes there?"

I stood very straight, as tall as I could, so that the Creepers couldn't see that I was nervous. I said very loudly, "My name is Steve! I'm looking for the little Creeper I met in the woods the other day!"

"Go away, Steve!" the big Creeper shouted back. "You can't have our little Creeper!"

I dropped my backpack to the ground and held both my hands up in the air so that the Creepers could see there was nothing in them. "I'm unarmed! I just want to talk!"

"Go away!" More Creepers began to shout. Several of them began to hiss, the sound that meant they were ready to explode.

"Easy, now," I said. "I don't want any trouble."

"It's too late for that!" said the biggest Creeper. All at once, several of the larger Creepers began rushing up the side of the quarry, hissing. As they got closer to me, they exploded. The sound was deafening: BOOM! BOOM! BOOM! Gravel and pieces of stone flew everywhere.

So I ran. I ran away as fast as I could, and I ran until I was certain that none of the Creepers were following me.

My plan failed, diary. The Creepers don't want to talk, and they don't want me to talk to the little friendly Creeper.

Tomorrow, I'm just going to go home. We'll have to make a new plan, I guess.

Day 193

Dear Diary,

You know, sometimes things work out in funny ways. Even though I had only talked to that friendly little Creeper once, in my mind I was already thinking of him as a friend. Turns out I wasn't the only one!

This morning, I woke up in a tree, climbed down, and started back toward the city. It wouldn't have taken me very long to get home; even though I was wandering through the woods for two days, I could just keep walking straight until I was out of the forest.

In fact, I was nearly there when I came across the strangest sight I'd ever seen. (And that's stranger than a cave full of zombies, an underground village, and a friendly Creeper, mind you!)

It was the family of three pigs again. But they weren't alone; there was a wolf with them, and a very small chicken was riding on the wolf's head!

"Oh, hello again!" said the father pig.

"Uh, hi," I said. "How are you?"

"We'd love to chat," said the wolf in a gruff voice, "but we have to go save our friend."

"Wait a second," the father pig said. "Weren't you looking for the friendly Creeper?"

"Yes, I was," I said, "but the other Creepers ran me off before I could talk to him."

"Well, we're going to save him right now!" said mama pig. She quickly explained that just this morning, the big Creepers had taken the little Creeper to a nearby village for him to prove he could explode like a real Creeper. But the villagers there had captured the little Creeper, and were keeping him in a cage!

"What about the other Creepers? Won't they help him?" I asked.

The little chicken shook her head. "They ran away. That's why we're going to save him."

"Then I'm coming with you," I said. "But we'll need some help. Wait here; I'll be right back!"

If we were going to save Friendly Creeper—which is what I had started calling him, in my mind—we would need help. I didn't have enough time to get Felicia or Charlie. But you can probably guess who I went and got, diary!

Twenty minutes later, the three pigs, the wolf, the chicken, me, and Burt the Golem made our way through the woods to the small village nearby. The wolf led, because he knew the shortcut to get there. The chicken rode on his head.

This particular village was very small, and the homes were all made of sandy brown stone. It must have looked very strange for the people there to see the "parade" of all of us walking right past their homes! And sure enough, there was a crowd of people in the village square gathered around an iron cage—and inside the cage was a very small, very scared Creeper.

"Release the little Creeper," Burt the Golem rumbled loudly. "That one is innocent."

The villagers all turned in surprise. A tall man shouted, "We caught him trying to blow up a house!"

"Oh, let him go, you big meanies!" the little chicken chirped from atop the wolf's head. "He's a friendly Creeper! Can't you see how scared he is?"

Finally I stepped forward. A few people gasped. I guess they knew who I was. Now, like I said earlier, I don't usually like the rumors that have spread about me, but sometimes they do some good.

"I am Minecraft Steve!" I said loudly. "And I order you to release that Creeper! He is my friend, and you are mistreating him! Now open that cage!"

The tall villager must have been very brave, because he stepped forward and said, "Or what?"

I smirked. "Or my iron golem here will release him for you." Golem grunted beside me to show them that we meant business.

That did it. The villagers quickly released Friendly Creeper, who hurried over to us. He thanked all of his animal friends, and then he turned to me. I guess he didn't know what to say, because he kind of stood there, looking embarrassed.

"How about we all go back to my castle?" I said. "I have cake!" (Which was half-true; I didn't actually have cake, but we did have a really great baker who could make us a cake in no time at all.)

And that, diary, is how three pigs, a wolf, a tiny chicken, an iron golem, and a very Friendly Creeper ended up at my pad for an awesome party.

Day 196

Dear Diary,

Phew! What a crazy few days it's been. Let me tell you what happened…

Felicia and Charlie became very fast friends with Friendly Creeper, but it wasn't easy convincing Mr. Mayor to let him stay in the city. People were still very scared after all the damage that was done. But me and Felicia did an excellent job rebuilding, and we haven't seen a single Creeper since. Besides, once anyone actually talks with FC (that's my nickname for him; it's easier than Friendly

Creeper), they realize he's a really nice fellow, and doesn't want to harm anyone.

FC decided that he would split his time between the city, and the Creepers; after all, they are technically his family, even if they don't treat him very nicely. But hey, friends support each other, so I told him that he's welcome at me and Charlie's pad anytime he wants.

Here's the best part: FC solved our Creeper problem in a way that was much better than what I had planned. When the other Creepers asked him how he got free from the villagers' cage, he told them I had charged in there with *ten* iron golems, and had threatened to destroy the whole village!

After that, the Creepers decided that our city was not a very good place to go. They think we have a golem army ready to toss any Creepers right out on their green behinds! And best of all, since they know that FC and I are now good friends, they don't mess with him as much as they used to.

Where I come from, there's another saying that goes, "All's well that ends well." That means that if something has a good ending, it doesn't matter if some bad things happened along the way. I think that sums up my last week or so perfectly.

Well, good night, diary. Tomorrow is a new day, and a new adventure!

Day 196 (part 2)

Dear Diary,

I can't believe I almost forgot to tell you! Remember I asked Felicia to ask around about those strange structures we saw? Well, she did—in fact, she went even further, and sent messengers to other cities and villages. Turns out that the guy who built them just recently came forward to tell people it was him.

His name is Herobrine. (I know, isn't that the weirdest name you ever heard?) He used to be a miner, but now he wants to be a builder. Apparently he lives out in the middle of nowhere in a little cabin by himself. If you think that's odd, there's more—people say he's not a very nice guy.

I'm not sure what they mean by that, but either way, I still want to meet him. I hope to get the chance soon!

Anyway, good night, diary!

THE END

Sneak Preview Of Diary Of A Minecrafting

Steve 4: The Better Builder

When a mysterious arch appears in the town the whole village is in a tizzy as to who built it. At first people think it's Minecraft Steve, but he knows it wasn't him. Before long though, the true builder reveals himself and … it's Herobrine! Not only did he build the arch, but he announces that he intends to become Minecraft Steve's greatest nemesis! Will Steve find the courage to meet this challenge? Read this illustrated short story to find out!

Day 1

Dear Diary,

Today is a great day. Do you want to know why? Because it's New Diary Day!

Let's see... I think you're now the fourth diary I've kept since I've come to this city. Each time I fill one up, I start a new one, and now it's your turn!

I started writing these diaries for two reasons: The first was to write down all the awesome adventures I have here in Minecraft... and there certainly have been a lot of them. The second reason was to keep track of how long I've been here. And, I'm ashamed to say, I've kind of lost track, which is why I've decided to start fresh with you as Day 1. Let's call it the start of a new adventure, okay?

The reason I lost track of time was because of all the cool stuff that's been going on the last couple of months. Let me give you the short version: When I came to this city, it was just a tiny village made of little gray cubes. I'm a builder—and a pretty good one, if I may say so myself—so I helped them out by building up this place into an awesome city. I had some help, of course; Felicia, one of my best friends, is also a really good builder (maybe even as good as me, but I probably wouldn't admit that to anyone except you, diary).

Word started spreading that I had built up this village into a city, so all sorts of other places started asking for our help. So the last couple of months, me and Felicia have been traveling around and helping to build neat new stuff all over the land.

Our other friend, Charlie the Chicken, usually comes with us when we go on our adventures. Charlie is a great pal, but he's not particularly useful when it comes to building—after all, he has wings, not hands—but a talking chicken is pretty good company. Sometimes our other friend, Friendly Creeper, will come with us too, but not always, because even though he's friendly, he's still a Creeper, and that tends to make people uncomfortable, on account of the way that Creepers usually like to explode.

Anyway, we've been having all sorts of adventures for the past couple of months, and since I've been away for so long, I filled up my last diary and lost track of time. It hasn't been a full year yet that I came here from "that other place" (which I don't like to talk about, so don't ask!) but I know it's been a while.

It's been long enough for people all over the land to hear about me and my friends. In fact, they've given me a nickname. They call me Minecraft Steve, on account of how good I am at building. But even though everyone thinks I'm this big hero, in my head I'm still just regular Steve. That's why I like having my friends around; they know the real me and they don't look at me the same way as everyone else… which is good, because it's a lot of pressure when you have to act like a hero all the time!

Today we finally got back home to our city after spending a few weeks helping a village on the other side of the woods. It was so good to be home! My pad—which is what I call my home—is actually a castle that I built when I had some spare time, and Charlie lives there with me. Felicia has her own house that's not too far away. Man, it was good to see the pad again! It's the best place in the world to kick back and relax.

We were greeted by Mr. Mayor, the white-haired mayor of our city, and my iron golem, who I've named Burt. (He's a really good protector and keeps an eye on my pad in case any Creepers or zombies show up, but he's also kind of grumpy-looking. I think he looks like a Burt.)

After we shared the stories of our adventure and got some pizza (bacon and pineapple, yum) I came right home to the pad to relax and start a new diary… which is where you come in.

Now that you're all caught up, I think I'm going to get some sleep. Tomorrow is a new day, and I can't wait to see what new adventures are in store for us next!

Day 2

Dear Diary,

...There was no adventure today. It was actually a pretty ordinary day. I woke up, had some breakfast, and walked the short distance into the city. My pad is up on a hillside that overlooks the town, so I can see everything that's going on just by looking out my window.

There wasn't anything interesting going on in town, so me and Charlie spent the day lounging around and trying to come up with something fun to do. It went something like this...

"Hey, Charlie, do you want to build a tree house?"

"Sure, Steve. We'll just need wood, and nails, and a tree…"

"Yeah, that sounds like a lot of work. Hey, do you want to have a pizza-eating contest?"

"No thanks. I had too much pizza yesterday. I'm pizza-pooped."

"Okay. Oh, hey, Charlie, do you want to make a canoe and paddle down the river?"

"I don't know, Steve, the water's really cold this time of year."

"Yeah, I guess you're right…"

You get the idea. So instead of adventure, we spent the day coming up with ideas for adventures.

I really hope something interesting happens soon!

Day 3

Dear Diary,

Still no adventure today. What gives? I'm Minecraft Steve. My life is supposed to be full of adventure. Maybe tomorrow, diary…

Day 4

Dear Diary,

Finally, something interesting happened! Sort of. Let me explain…

This morning I got up and had some breakfast, like I usually do. I said good morning to Burt, who just kind of grunted back to me, and then I tiptoed past Charlie's chicken coop (he likes to sleep in a little coop in the courtyard, even though my castle has like ten rooms). Then I walked down into the city to see if anything fun was going on.

I wasn't expecting it, because lately there hasn't been anything fun or interesting going around, so I was surprised to find that everyone was chatting excitedly. They were saying things like, "Have you seen it?" and "Where did it come from? Who could have done it?"

Then Mr. Mayor came running up to me, his gray beard blowing in the breeze. "Was it you? Did you do it?" he asked me quickly.

Of course, I had no idea what he was talking about, so I asked him, "What's *it*?"

"Let me show you! Come see!" and he ran off toward the edge of town. I followed him. Just outside the city, on the other side from where my pad is, was a crowd of people, and they were all looking at a strange structure.

It was an arch. It was made of gray stone. It wasn't really big, or bold, or bright... but it was beautiful. It was perfectly smooth with rounded edges, and it was set up in a way that made it look like an entrance to our city.

I hate to admit it, diary, but it might have been the nicest thing I've ever seen built in all of Minecraft! It was so simple, but so well made that... well, it made me kind of jealous.

And to top it all off, all of the people from our city that were crowded around it were "oohing" and "aahing" at it like it was the best thing they'd ever seen! I stepped closer to it and touched it. The edges were so smooth and round! The curve was perfect! *How?* I thought. *How could someone have made this, and in just one night?*

And diary, since you're the keeper of my secrets, I'll tell you a big one: My jealousy started to turn into anger. I got mad. Someone was building in *my* city! *I'm* supposed to be the builder here! If you look around this place, you'll see all the great stuff I've done (with some help, of course). And this person comes along and just decides to build an arch? Why?

"I think I know who did this," Felicia said quietly. I jumped a little. I had no idea that she had come to see the arch; in fact, she was standing right beside me, like a sneaky little ninja.

"Who?" I asked.

"I bet it was Herobrine."

I sort of remembered hearing the name before— mostly because it's a strange name, and not one you're likely to forget—but I couldn't remember where I'd heard it. "Who's that again?"

Felicia rolled her eyes. "Don't you remember? You asked me to find out who was building all those strange random structures we saw, and I told you—it was a miner named Herobrine."

"Oh, right." With everything that we'd been doing the last couple of months, I'd kind of forgotten all about that. "But why would he build here?"

Felicia shrugged. "Maybe he's challenging you."

I get a sinking feeling in my stomach. Don't get me wrong, I'm all for a challenge, but this arch... it's perfect. I don't think I could build anything quite like this.

"Anyway," Felicia said, "People say Herobrine is kind of a jerk. But wow, he can build. I mean, look at this thing! It's awesome."

"It's not *that* great," I tell her, feeling that angry feeling again. All of the people in the city getting excited over it, and now Felicia too?

After that, I decided to go back to my pad. I didn't really want to be around people, because all they wanted to talk about was the arch and how amazing it was. Even Charlie flapped into my room later in the afternoon. "Steve!" he said excitedly. "Did you see it?"

"Yes, Charlie, I saw it," I said flatly.

"It's great—"

"Yeah, it's great!" I snapped at him. "Now go away."

Charlie looked kind of hurt, but he wandered off on his little chicken feet. I didn't mean to be mean to him, but I was already tired of hearing people talk about the arch.

What if this Herobrine guy really is a better builder than me? And what if Felicia is right and his arch is his way of challenging me?

All in one afternoon I went from jealous to angry to uncertain. The confidence I have in my building abilities comes mostly from all these people telling me how great I am, but the truth is… where I come from—that place I don't like to talk about—I'm *not* the best builder, diary. I mean, I'm pretty good, but there are people that are way better.

And then I have the worst thought of all: What if Herobrine comes from another place too?

I wandered around my castle for a while, and it helped gain some of my confidence back. I mean, my pad is awesome. And then I got an idea. Maybe I don't have to worry about Herobrine. Maybe I can build something so

great, so magnificent, that people will remember who the

real builder is around here, and Herobrine will lose *his*

confidence! That's a solid plan, right diary?

So I'm going to get to work. I have to draw up
some plans!

Click HERE to download the rest of the

story now!

Special Free Comics Offer From Funny Comics

Funny Comics is the leading publisher of funny stories, comics and graphic novels on the web. Make sure to "LIKE" our fan page on Facebook below:

https://www.facebook.com/FunnyComics3000

On this page we will share news on everything we are up to as well as notify you when our comics are available for FREE on Kindle.

Other Comics And Short Stories From Funny Comics

How To Train Your Ender Dragon Series
In this series of illustrated short stories Steve Montgomery is your typical 15 year old kid with 15 year old problems. However, there is one unusual thing about him. Steve Montgomery has the power to summon dragons ...

How To Train Your Ender Dragon

Steve Montgomery is your typical 15 year old with 15
year old problems. The biggest of which is that he is
often bullied by a group of kids that includes his own
brother. Steve has something that most other kids
don't have, however, for he has the power to summon
dragons. After he is literally strung up a flagpole by
his tormentors Steve meets a magical dragon who not
only saves him but whisks him away to the magical
world of Minecraft. However once he arrives there he
soon learns that other dangers exist besides school
bullies. ...

Diary Of A Minecrafting Steve Series

To everyone who knows him, he is the great Minecraft Steve, the greatest builder the world has ever known. People see him as brave, creative and a natural born leader. Too bad he doesn't feel that way! Follow Steve's journey as he faces his fears and learns along the way that he just might be a hero after all.

Diary Of A Minecrafting Steve – Zombies Don't Eat Chicken

Minecraft Steve arrives in a new village and it's everything he hopes it will be. He wants to be a builder, and this village needs building! What's more everyone looks up to Steve as he doesn't appear to be afraid of anything, although deep down Steve knows this isn't true. He's actually afraid of many things, especially zombies! This doesn't concern him very much until he learns that a bunch of zombies may have kidnapped his friend. Can Steve find the courage to overcome his fears, or will he lose his friend forever? Read this engaging illustrated short story to find out!

The Adventures Of Fartman Series
In this series of illustrated short stories you will thrill to the adventures of Minecraft's greatest hero, Fartman! Armed only with the power of his farts read along as Fartman works to protect his home and friends from the schemes of the evil Enderman!
In this series of illustrated short stories you will get to experience life from Herobrine's point of view. Is Herobrine really bad, or just misunderstood?

The Adventures Of Fartman – The Beginning

Steve has a problem. He farts. He farts like no one has ever farted. He farts so badly that it's hard for him to make friends or even hold a job. However when the village he lives in is threatened by the nefarious Enderman Steve starts to see his farting curse as a potential gift. Read this story and witness as he transforms himself from mild mannered Steve into the mighty Fart Man!

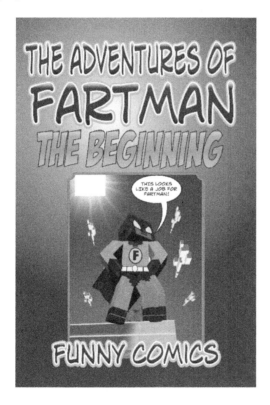

Herobrine's Diary Series
In this series of illustrated short stories you will get to experience life from Herobrine's point of view. Is Herobrine really bad, or just misunderstood?

Herobrine's Diary 1: It Ain't Easy Being Mean

Everyone knows Herobrine is the villain in Minecraft, but was it always this way? What's more, how did Herobrine get this way to begin with? In this illustrated short story Herobrine tells all from his perspective. At first he really only wanted to build things and help people. However, everyone he meets just won't accept him at his word. Maybe being a bad guy isn't that bad after all?

Big & Little Buddy's Time Traveling Stories
In this series of illustrated short stories the greatest
inventors in Minecraft, Big and Little Buddy, travel
through time in order to stop Herobrine. You see,
Herorbine is a time traveller too, although he wants to
change the past so that he can rule the future! With
the help of their friends such as Steve and Friendly
Creeper, the dynamic duo meet several important
historical figures and have fun all the while thwarting
Herobrine's time warping schemes!

Tear Down This Wall!

Minecraft Steve arrives at the home of his favorite inventors, Big Buddy and Little Buddy. He hopes to see their latest inventions. What he doesn't expect though is for their entire lab to vanish into a corn field!

Big Buddy quickly determines that something has gone wrong in the timeline, and it's up to them to fix it! Steve doesn't want to go, but Little Buddy drags him along. Before you know it the trio are travelling back in time to East Germany to figure out what has gone wrong. To their surprise, the Berlin Wall is still standing and Ronald Reagan never became president of the United States! Could Herorbine be behind these dastardly schemes and can he be stopped in time?

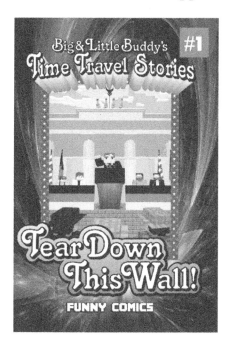

STEVE'S COMIC ADVENTURES Series

In this comic series Steve must use the power of his imagination in order to defeat the evil plans of Herobrine. We've based stories so far on Jurassic Park, Star Wars and The Wizard Of Oz. More to come!

Steve's Comic Adventures: Jurassic Block

Steve's Comic Adventures: Attack On The Death Square

1

Steve's Comic Adventures: That's How You Get Ants, Man!

Minecraft Steve Adventures – The Craving Games

In this illustrated short story Minecraft Steve must use his knowledge of the Hunger Games to defeat Herorbine!

The Adventures Of Big Buddy And Little Buddy Series

In this comic series Big Buddy and Little Buddy are friends, inventors and adventurers. Big Buddy tends to be more serious and practical. Little Buddy? Let's just say a little less so. Nonetheless they always have each other's back no matter what trouble they get into!

Reviewers and Friends of Funny Comics Hall of FAME – We LOVE YOU!

As a small, independent publisher we are EXTREMELY appreciative of our fans. The people listed below have either consistently reviewed our books and comics on Amazon or have offered us story ideas / comments to us through the e-mail listed below. This is fantastic as it helps us make our stories better. . We REALLY appreciate your reviews, thoughts and ideas. If you feel like you should be featured in our honor roll below please contact us via our e-mail address. In the meantime here is a list of the people who have really supported us in the past. THANK-YOU ONE AND ALL!

W. Shi – New York City

Stephanie Linn

May Ong – Singapore

Patrick Jane – Orlando

Lin

WD

Hannah

Funnycomics1@gmail.com

Thank-you again for reading our story and we hope you enjoyed it!

Please Help Us Make Our Comics And

Short Stories Better!

If you enjoy our comics and short stories could you do us a favor and please leave a review on Amazon for them? We gauge a series popularity but how popular it is with our reviewers and readers. The more positive reviews the more likely we are to make more short stories and / or comics in that series. Also, we love hearing from our fans. If you have any ideas / suggestions or improvements please write to us at the e-mail address below. It could be anything. Story ideas, suggestions for improvement, etc. We are thinking about rewarding the top ideas and / or suggestions by perhaps making you a character in a future story. This is only an idea, but we are seriously thinking about it. Anyway, our e-mail address is below:

Funnycomics1@gmail.com

Thank-you again for reading our story and we hope you enjoyed it!

Made in the USA
Monee, IL
27 February 2021